PRODIGIOUS
WORLDS
THE FIRST WORLDS

Also available in eBook.

Published by Dark Titan Publishing. A division of Dark Titan Entertainment.

Prodigious Worlds is an imprint of Dark Titan Entertainment.

Paperback ISBN: 979-8-9866393-0-7
eBook ISBN: 979-8-9866393-1-4

darktitanentertainment.com

WORKS BY TY'RON W. C. ROBINSON II

BOOKS/SHORT STORIES

DARK TITAN UNIVERSE SAGA

MAIN SERIES
Dark Titan Knights
The Resistance Protocol
Tales of the Scattered
Tales of the Numinous
Day of Octagon
Crossbreed
Heaven's Called
The Oranos Imperative
Underworld

COLLECTIONS
Dark Titan Omnibus: Volume 1
Dark Titan Omnibus: Volume 2
Dark Titan One-Shot Collection
Dark Titan One-Shot Collection II
Dark Titan Universe Saga Spin-offs
Omnibus: Volume 1

SPIN-OFFS
In A Glass of Dawn: The Casebook of
Travis Vail
Maveth: Bloodsport
The Curse of The Mutant-Thing
Trail of Vengeance
War of The Thunder Gods
The Trials of Shade & Switchblade

ONE-SHOTS
Maveth, The Death-Bringer
Mystery of The Mutant-Thing
Shade & Switchblade
Retribution of Cain
The Mythologists
Ambush Bot
Kang-Zhu
Cheeseburger Man
Tessa Balthazar
Elite 5
Peacekeeper

THE HAUNTED CITY SAGA
The Legendary Warslinger: The Haunted City I
Battle of Astolat: A Haunted City Prequel (KOBO Exclusive)
Redemption of the Lost: The Haunted City II
Helper's Hand: A Haunted City One-Shot

SYMBOLUM VENATORES
Symbolum Venatores: The Gabriel Kane Collection
Hod: A Symbolum Venatores Book
Symbolum Venatores: War of The Two Kingdoms
Symbolum Venatores: Elrad's Chronicles

EVERWAR UNIVERSE
EverWar Universe: Knights & Lords
EverWar Universe: Avior vs. Dekar

PRODIGIOUS WORLDS
Mark Porter of Argoron
Raiders of Vanok
Praxus of Lithonia

FRIGHTENED! SERIES
Frightened!: The Beginning

INSTINCTS SERIES
Lost in Shadows: Remastered
Instincts Point Hope

DARK TITAN'S THE DEAD DAYS
Accounts of The Dead Days

THE HORDE TRILOGY
The Horde
The Dreaded Ones

OTHER BOOKS
The Book of The Elect
The Extended Age Omnibus
The Eleventh Hour: A Chevah Mythos Story
The Supreme Pursuer: Darkness of the Hunt
Massacre in the Dusk
Venture into Horror: Tales of the Supernatural
The Universe of Realms Omnibus: Book 1
The Universe of Realms Omnibus: Book 2

THE DARK TITAN AUDIO EXPERIENCE PODCAST
Season 1: Introductions
Season 2: In a Glass of Dawn
Season 2.5: Accounts of The Dead Days
Season 3: Battle For Astolat
Season 4: Hallow Sword: Cursed

PRODIGIOUS WORLDS

THE FIRST WORLDS

TYRON W. C. ROBINSON II

CONTENTS

MARK PORTER OF ARGORON

CHAPTER 1: THE INCIDENT

United States Army Lieutenant, Mark Porter is currently on a mission to Roswell, New Mexico. His focus is keen as he traveled alone, listening to musical instrumentals. As he drove, his cell phone rings and he answers it.

"Lieutenant Porter." he said.

"Porter, this is General Dunlap." the caller said. "How far are you from the site?"

"I'm looking at it as we speak." Porter said.

Porter drove to the entrance gate, where two soldiers stood. They opened the gate , permitting him entry. Porter recognized the location, while still speaking with the General on the phone.

"General, I must ask, what is this place?"

"This is Area 51."

"Area 51." Porter intrigued. "I never thought I would be here."

"See you inside, Porter."

Porter hung up the phone, entering into the front entrance of the buildings. Area 51 had the appearance of a small city, with dozens of soldiers and officials moving throughout. Most of which are military soldiers and scientists. Porter stepped out of the car, heading towards the front doors layered with bulletproof glass. He entered, being greeted by soldiers. Porter took a left turn toward the elevator. Inside the elevator were two scientists.

"Excuse me, but are you Mark Porter?" one scientist asked.

"Yes I am."

"Its an honor to meet such a well-known Lieutenant." the other scientist said.

"Thank you."

The elevator had reached its destination floor. Porter is the first one to walk out, only to avoid the two scientists. Porter walked down a hallway and in the distance, he saw General Dunlap. Porter begins walking toward him. General Dunlap saw Porter coming down the hall near him.

"Porter, right on schedule."

"Yes sir, General."

Porter and General Dunlap entered another room. As they walked, Dunlap began telling Porter a few details to the secret operations being held within the facility. Porter took a guess to what it may be with only Dunlap smirking without saying a word.

"Porter, there are some rules that you must obey, since you're here."

"Ok, General. What are they?"

"You must not tell a single soul what you're about to see in this next room." Dunlap said. "If you do, we will have no choice but to rid you of the world."

"I see. Must be something very important."

"Important?" Dunlap said. "Try highly secretive. If anyone found out about this, the world will turn for the worst."

They reached the room and the metal door slowly slides open. The room was surrounded with military security. Little light was emitted into the room as the rest was covered in darkness. Porter gazed around, seeing scientists doing autopsies on unknown beings.

"General, what is going on here?" Porter asked.

"I'll tell you once we've reached our location."

Passing through the security, walking into yet another room. This room was lit up with plenty of light and wasn't nearly as shrouded in darkness like the other. Inside the room is a long table with a device

2

sitting in the middle. Porter and Dunlap approached the table, looking at the device.

"Porter, this device you see here is able to transfer beings, human or not, to other worlds."

"Other worlds? Like planets?"

"Yes. Perhaps even dimensions are a possibility. Testing will only reveal how soon."

"How is that possible?" Porter asked. "Has it been tested?"

"Not yet. We're still awaiting an answer from the President."

They walked around the table, looking from all angles. The device was shiny, projecting a blue light which directed into the air. Porter slowly held his hand over the device before Dunlap snatched it from getting closer.

"You don't want to do something that you'll regret."

"Sorry, sir."

As they stood looking at the device, an alarm goes off. Porter and Dunlap look around. Dunlap ran toward the doors, questioning the security as to what triggered the alarm.

"What the hell's going on?!" Dunlap yelled.

"The base, sir, its under attack!" a soldier yelled.

"Porter, stay where you are!"

He pulled out his pistol, looking outside the door. From the outside, he saw soldiers and scientists being attacked by an unknown force. The opposing force appeared to have tentacles, while wearing peculiar white robes with long white hair extending to their lower back. Dunlap glared out of the glass window of the door, staring at them, watching them kill the soldiers and scientists. Gunshots are heard from the outside, but they're dying left and right.

Porter approached toward the door, but is stopped by Dunlap, who commanded Porter to stay by the table.

"General, what's going on?!"

"Sit tight, Lieutenant!" Dunlap said. "We're in for a show."

Dunlap backed from the door as it bursts open. He began shooting at the beings, but the gunshots have no effect. Porter takes out his revolver and shoots one of the beings in the head, which kills it. Dunlap looks at Porter, astounded.

"Try that, General."

"I surely will."

They both begin shooting the beings that are coming into the room through the damaged door. They aim for the head and shoot them directly there. They've killed the beings and look at each other. Both astounded and calm.

"Good job, Lieutenant."

"Same to you, General."

They shook hands, but from the ceiling a bright light shines down on them and Porter pushes Dunlap out of the way and a loud bang is heard with a large flash of light, nearly blinding Dunlap. The light fades away and Dunlap looks around for Porter.

"Porter?" Dunlap spoke. "Porter?!"

Dunlap looks around and realizes that Porter is nowhere in sight, but he also realized that the device's light is now dim, which before it was bright. He now knows that someone has happened to Porter.

Porter, who's opening his eyes, realizes that he's in a desert. He looks and stands up, brushing the dirt off of his uniform. He walks around the area, looking around at it surroundings.

"Where the hell am I?"

CHAPTER 2: CAPTIVE FOREIGNER

He continued walking, although realizing that he can move faster and jump higher than usual. Knowing now something isn't quite right. He continued to move ahead, but in front of him, he sees something running towards him. He tries to get a closer look and he sees that they looked human. He begins running the other direction, but is shot down by a bow and arrow. Porter lays on the ground as the beings get closer to him. He now hears silence, but the beings are surrounding him.

The beings appeared to be humans, yet there was a difference to them. Their skin was darker and their bodies were toned. They stared down Porter as he glared at them. They spoke to each other in an unknown language that Porter couldn't understand. He stood up, staggering from the arrow wound, stepping back from the beings and points to the one wearing white fur over his shoulders. His stature gave Porter to belief to be the general.

"You, where am I? Tell me where the hell I am?!"

The humanoids looked at Porter, their thoughts ponder if he's not from their world. One approached Porter and looks at him from all angles and stands back with his group. Porter stares at the group, reaching for his revolver, but he doesn't have it. He looks at what he perceived to be the humanoids' general and saw he had his revolver.

"How did you get that?!" Porter asked with rage. "Where am I?!"

Porter walked over to the beings, but he's knocked unconscious by one of their punches. They dragged him back to their location, locking him up. Hours later, Porter awakens and is now chained to a rock with no way out. He sees the beings from before, but this time, there's more. Porter begins thinking that he may not be on Earth anymore. He know believes that he's somewhere else, somewhere unknown.

Porter tried to break himself out of the chains, but he's too tired and weary to do so. He looks around as he's surrounded by dirt and feces. He continues to look around to find an object that could break him out of the chains. He doesn't find any tools that he could use, so he sits in the dungeon through the entire night. The next day, he awakens and sees himself surrounded by the tall, green beings. One in particular, releases him of the chains and helps him up, Porter stares at the being and looks into its eyes.

"What are you?" Porter asked.

"We are the Micrans." The being said. "Warriors of Argoron."

"What…? Argoron? Where am I?"

"You are on Argoron, stranger."

"Argoron?' Porter said. 'Where is that? I've never heard of Argoron.'

"If you're not from here, then, where do you come from?.' The being said. "What is your origin?"

"I'm not understanding what you mean? Where exactly am I?"

"You're on Argoron. A planet in the vastness of the stars."

"Argoron?" Porter questioned. "No. I was just in New Mexico."

"Where do you come from? Truly?"

"My name is Mark Porter." Porter said. "."

From the entrance came the leader of this particular warrior clan, Saban Jai. Saban walked toward and stood in front of Porter. Porter stared, not knowing what to expect.

"Mark Porter." Saban said. "How can you be from Jagoron?"

"What? No, I'm from Earth, not Jagoron? What is a Jagoron?"

"That is what I said, Mark Porter of Jagoron The world you come from is called Jagoron in this land. To your species, the earth-walkers, Jagoron is called Earth."

Porter sat confused. The Micrans didn't know what to make of his reaction. Saban didn't bother with him, rallying the others to bring him to the carriage. The carriage seemed to be made of a reddish wood as were the wheels, decorated with spears and red flags with no markings. Two of the Micrans carried Porter into the carriage, which was pulled by two eight-legged creatures. Which Porter saw them, he immediately thought them to be horses. However, he spotted they each had two tails and two sets of eyes on both sides. Speaking the word, Saban chuckled.

"Moreks." Saban said. "That's what they are. The fastest beasts in all of Argoron."

Saban jumped into the front of the carriage, gaining control over the horses as they rode off from the vast desert toward the massive metropolitan city as they approached the gates of the city of *Taranopolis*, as the inhabitants called it. Porter took a look outside of the carriage, seeing the massive city with its pointed skyscrapers and layered structures. The vehicles which moved throughout the city were a mix of the carriage and anti-gravity ships. The ships appeared to have four sets of transparent wings in the colors of rubies. The sky above the city was orange with a hint of red. The city was surrounded by red flags, flowing calmly with the wind throughout the city as the temperature was warm enough to have the people dressed in light clothing. Some even glanced at Porter, seeing his attire. From there, Porter knew he was out of place, especially when glancing upward toward the ships.

"Where am I?" Porter asked himself.

The carriage stopped in front of the city's palace. The Micrans stood by the carriage door, dragging Porter to the outside as they entered the palace. Porter stood on his feet, being held by two Micran soldiers, walking toward what he guessed was the throne room. In the room, Porter saw three chairs. Two were empty and the center one was full as there was a man sitting, speaking with another man. The man standing up had the wings of a dragon folded on his back and claws for fingers. Dressed in armored leather. The man sitting down was decked in armor, linen, and fur. On his head sat a crown made of what appeared to be gold or bronze. Porter couldn't make out any of it, yet, he knew they were royalty in their own way.

"You know why I've come and visited you, my lord."

"Yes, I am aware of your need for warriors. As of right now, there aren't many who are at my disposal for combat."

"What of your prisoners? What use will you have for them other than wasting away behind cell doors?"

The one in the chair nodded, rubbing his chin.

"You have a point."

They looked toward the entrance, seeing the Micrans carrying Porter. The man standing pointed and his yellow eyes widen. The man in the seat stood up, glaring toward the Micran warriors and the prisoner they held.

"A new prisoner?"

"My lord." Saban said, kneeling. "We have another prisoner in need of interrogation."

The man stared at Porter, seeing his clothing and his tone. He was uncertain of Porter's ethnicity to his own and the others around him. He turned back to Saban, raising his hand, giving him the order to stand.

"And what has this man done and what is he wearing?"

"We're not sure, sire. He was dressed in this manner when we found him."

"And where did you find him?"

"Out in the wilderness. He appeared dazed. Confused you might say. He was speaking strangely, so we brought him here. To get more answers. If you request it, my king."

The King nodded.

"Very well. Take him to the room. Ivo will be there to get any answers we may need."

"And what of him after you received your answers?" The other man said.

"When the time comes, I will call to you, Wyvern King. Right now, best you return to your domain. Prepare your warriors for the entertainment of the masses."

"I will keep my eyes and ears open."

The Wyvern King's wings buckled as he nodded his head, walking toward the exit. The King looked back, seeing Saban and the warriors leading Porter into the interrogation room. He sighed as he sat down and from the entrance arrived a young woman, dressed in a silver dress and long reddish-orange hair. She bowed before the king and he smiled.

"My daughter. I see you've returned from your journey."

"I have, father. I also have some news regarding the people of the city."

"News? What kind of news?"

"The people are aware of the coming war with the Celedians."

"And how do they know this?"

"Some have described a strange man coming into the city, warning them of the war and giving them the choice to choose which side they're on."

"A speaker of war in my city." The King said. "I see I must find him. Or, perhaps Saban has already brought him in."

The Princess wasn't sure what her father had meant. He chuckled and stood up, walking toward his daughter.

"Let me handle the matters of war. You must prepare for a wedding. Saban is a good man and a future leader."

"I… I understand."

The King looked at his daughter as she let out a small smile.

"I have other matters to attend to. Make sure you keep yourself protected when you're out in the city."

"The guardsmen will stand by me."

"Good, my Arribel."

CHAPTER 3: WHO ARE YOU?

Porter struggled against the strength of the two Micrans as they chained his wrists to the wall before exiting. Porter stared quietly, hearing footsteps approaching the cell. The door had opened for Porter to glance at two other warriors and a peculiar following the middle. He stood about the height of Porter, but he was much older as his white hair could attest.

"Who are you?"

"What?" Porter said slowly.

"Who are you? What is your name?"

"My name is Mark Porter."

"Mark Porter." Ivo said. "Strange name. never heard of such a one. Tell me, Mark Porter, where are you from?"

"I'm not from here. So, that's a start."

"Your name tells me all I need to know. Why have you come here, Mark Porter? Are you a spy for the Celedians? The Ceruleanians? Orgons, perhaps?"

"What are you talking about? I'm not from this place. "

"Your physical tells the tale. You're a warrior."

"I'm a soldier. A lieutenant."

"Convenient." Ivo chuckled. "And you've come here for what purpose other than being a spy or an invader?"

"I am not an invader nor am I some kind of spy. I didn't come here on my own accord. It's hard to explain. Even for myself. The place I come from is Earth. Earth is my home."

"Earth? You speak of Jagoron, the blue world where the waters move across the grounds."

"I guess you can detail it as much."

"Who sent you here?"

"I don't know."

"Then, start with something for me to go along. To understand your plight."

Porter sighed, waving his hands slight in a non-caring manner, yet, Porter began to tell Ivo of the encounter in Area 51, the ambush, and the instant transportation. Ivo listened closely to every word Porter had spoken. Once Porter had come to the conclusion of his sudden appearance in the desert, Ivo ceased him.

"You were brought here."

"Yes. But, I'm not sure by what or how."

"What is it you truly desire at this moment?"

"To be out of these chains and to be sent back home."

Ivo chuckled.

"There will be a time for that. Getting you back home however, is a tricky obstacle. For if you do not know how you came to Argoron, how does it make sense for you to find your way back."

"I saw the ships you people have. They're far beyond what I've seen. Now, I can take one of them and fly it back to Earth. A safe passage to get home."

"Enough." Ivo said, silencing Porter. "Our customs are far different than your kind. For one to achieve the freedom which one craves, they must earn it and win it."

"Win it? I'm not understanding."

"Combat. A trial to test your strength. To learn your endurance. Mentally. Physically. Spiritually. Only then will we and yourself see the conclusion to the whole matter."

"Are you telling me I must fight to get home?"

"Yes."

Porter sighed. Hanging his head low. He thought for a moment if this was only a dream. A hallucination, yet, with the small pain he felt in his legs, he knew it was real. All of it.

"I'm sorry. But, I am not going to be treated as some sort of amusement to you and your people here. I demand to be sent home."

Ivo turned back and walked toward the cell door. He opened it before taking a look back at Porter. Measuring him with a gaze.

"Your freedom demands on your fighting spirit. I hope you have one."

Ivo exited the cell, calling over a Micran guard. Ivo signaled the guard to keep watch of Porter's cell for the remainder of the day and throughout the night. Several hours later, nightfall fell over Taranopolis and the city was sleep. The sky which as glowing red had become as dark with glares and glistens of a peculiar bluish hue. Porter sat inside his cell. Barely ate the food they delivered to him. He looked over toward the guard sitting at the door. With the faint light shining from the window above him, Porter caught the glimpse of a key. Believing the key to be the only way out of his cell. Porter made a move, but remembered his wrists were attached to chains embedded into the concrete wall.

"Hey." Porter whispered. "Hey."

The guard jolted a bit, no movement afterwards. Porter sighed as he looked around the cell for something. Anything to get the guard's attention. Porter thought and glanced over to his left, seeing the tray of food. His eyes moved from the tray to the guard. Porter swiped his foot, kicking the tray against the cell doors, rattling up the guard as he jumped up with a sword in hand. Porter saw the blade.

"What's going on in there?" The guard asked.

"Water." Porter said. " I need water."

"Water? Where do you see any water?"

"To drink. I need something to drink."

The guard sighed and walked off, leaving Porter waiting. Unsure of what he could've waited for, the guard had returned, holding a small flask in his hand. He opened the cell door and entered, putting the flask on the ground as he unlocked the cuff from Porter's right wrist from the chain. Porter sighed and paused, quickly snatching he flask and smashing it into the guard's face before kicking the guard in the throat and stomping on his head. The helmet which the guard had word was cracked on the side. Porter looked to the guard's hand, seeing the key. He grabbed it and unruffled his left wrist. Being free from the wall, Porter grabbed the chest plate and helmet of the guard. Taking the sword last as he made his escape from the cell. Porter moved through the corridors quietly, avoiding other guards and even those who were playing a game of *L'agh*. In the distance, Porter saw the moonlight peaking from a doorway. Porter reached the door and found himself staring at the outside toward the vast desert. He sighed, knowing if he wanted to escape, going back into the desert was his only option. Porter made his move and ran out into the desert with only Argoron's moon as his source of direction.

CHAPTER 4: THE FLYING MEN

Porter had went afar out into the desert, he even glanced back and could only see the tips from the skyscrapers which stood in Taranopolis. Gasping for breath and of thirst, Porter continued walking. Even in the chilling cold. The air was almost below freezing to Porter's understanding. As he walked, he took a gaze up into the sky, seeing the peaking sun hovering behind a set of clouds. The heat began o rise throughout the desert sands as Porter continues trekking along the dunes around him. No sign of life. No animals. No plants. Porter walked alone in the desert.

From there, he came to a stop at what he believed to be a entry into some kind of cavern. Exhaling from the long walk, Porter approached the entry point, discovering the entrance into a small cave. He stepped forward to the cave and let out a faint shout. Nothing responded. He took the time to sit down and relax himself. He closed his eyes and calmly breathed. Afterwards, he heard what he believed to be something running within the cavern. Using his remaining strength to stand, Porter entered the cavern deeper and found a small pond which was set by a waterfall within the cavern. Pleased, Porter ran over into the pond, soaking himself in the water. He went and drank from the waterfall. In a strangeness to him, the water was cool. Near icy.

"Where does this water come from in a place such as this?" Porter thought to himself.

Taking several minutes to relax himself within the pond. He stepped from it and returned to the entry point. Once he saw the sand in the distance, he caught three shadows in the sand. Hearing the wind above him. Porter ran out to see what was in the air and what he had seen were the wyvern men. Half-man and half-wyvern. Their bodies from their head to their waist were similar to a man. Yet, their legs and wings were of wyverns. Porter went and hid in the cavern, but one of the wyvern men caught him as he sat back against the rock wall. The wyvern man flew down to the cavern as Porter remained silent.

"Whatever you are," The wyvern man said. "Come out and face us."

Porter sighed in regret and slowly took his steps out of the cavern for the wyvern man to see. Unknown to Porter of the wyvern man's height. He stood over Porter by nine-feet and a half. The second wyvern man flew down, standing besides his partner as they stared at Porter. Seeing his garb. They were dumfounded.

"You're a strange one."

"I'm strange?" Porter said. "Look at the two of you. Hybrid beasts."

"What do they call you?" The wyvern man asked.

"My name?"

"Do you have one?"

"Mark Porter."

"Very well, Mark Porter. Myself and my colleague are elite soldiers for the Wyvern King. This cavern and the water within belong to him and him alone."

Porter chuckled.

"You're saying this king of yours owns this?"

"Precisely. As of this moment, you are trespassing."

"Listen, this is the best place I've come to so far on this planet or wherever the hell I am. Now, I am going to give the two of you to the count of three to leave me alone. Go fly up and bother someone else."

"You are not authorized to give us orders."

"I just did. What are you going to do with them?"

The second wyvern man looked over to his partner. Pointing at Porter's body. Noticing his demeanor and attitude. The first wyvern man took notice and nodded before turning his gaze toward Porter.

"If you won't leave our king's cave, then we must take you to him."

Porter balled his fists and clashed them. Standing tall before the wyvern men. They looked to one another and only came to a silent agreement. Before Porter to throw a punch, the wyvern men tackled him, stomping him into the sand. Porter tried to block the stomps with his arms, but one of the stomps collided with his head and chest, knocking him inconspicuous. Once the wyvern men knew of Porter's current status, they agreed to take him and they did. Carrying him in the air as they flew back to their place of origin.

CHAPTER 5: FINDING THE WARRIOR

Within Taranopolis the same day and hour, the guards searched the city searching for Porter under the orders of King R'akl. The guards returned to him, informing him of Porter's disappearance and lack of trace in the city region. King R'akl wondered how Porter made his escape in the night and several guards approached the king, detailing in of the discovery of a dead guard in the cell where Porter was kept. With murder being the case, R'akl called for a manhunt on Porter to be searched out and arrested on sight. The guards took in the king's command and headed out to find Porter even outside the city region. Princess Lola approached her father with caution, asking for alternative ways to find Porter. But, the king did not want to hear a word from his daughter regarding the foreign prisoner.

"What if he comes across the others? Like The Wyvern King?"

"If he does come across the Wyvern King, then the Wyvern King will bring him back to us. He knows our ways and if he doesn't want Micran warriors on his doorstep, then, he will return what is ours without haste."

"You know the Wyvern kind just as much as the rest of us. They will take whatever they can and use it for their own cause. If they come across him, they will use him against your kingdom. Against all of us under your command.

"Enough, my daughter." R'akl yelled. "Leave such matters to me. Right now, you should be concerning yourself with your upcoming marriage to Saban Jai. Focus on that and leave the duties of warfare to me. For these will become such matters for Saban when he is king."

"Yes, father." Lola replied, bowing before her father as she took her leave.

Leaving the palace, Lola commanded two guards to bring her one of the traveller-chariots. She instructed them to leave outside of the city gates. Unknown to her reasoning, they did not bother to question her, for she is the king's daughter and future wife to Saban Jai. Obeying her word, Lola arrived outside the gates, seeing the chariots. She stepped onto the chariot as one of her handmaidens approached. Getting on the chariot as well.

"What are you doing?" Lola asked.

"I'm coming with you. No need for you to travel out there alone."

"If we're caught, you'll be in serious trouble. Possibly banishment or death."

"I will do what I must for the future queen."

Lola nodded with uncertainty as they rode off into the desert. While riding in the desert, the handmaiden, who's name was Serai asked Lola where they were heading. Lola informed Serai she was heading to the landmass of the Hibarian Forest. Serai questioned why would Lola seek help inside the deep forest, Lola only responded by detailing they will need to speak to the dwellers who live within and without the forest.

After some time had passed, Lola looked ahead, seeing the palm-like trees in the distance. The Hibarian Forest was near. A land parallel to the desert. Lush with grass, flowing water and many, many trees. Trees standing nearly the height of Taranopolis' skyscrapers. Nearing the entrance to the forest, they are stopped by two figures. Standing over ten-feet tall. Their skin was as green as the grass and their eyes were as golden as the sand. Brute physiques and rough demeanors. Lola knew what they were as she raised her hands in the midst of them aiming their weapons toward her.

"I come not to bring trouble. I am looking for someone. Perhaps you might have seen him."

18

"We do not understand what you speak of."

"There was a prison who escaped Taranopolis. I have come to ask if you've seen the man."

"We've seen no Micran."

"This man is not a Micran. He is something else. Beyond Argoron.

From the trees behind the guards came forward another one of their kind, yet covered in fur and jewelry. The two guards knelt down before him.

"Princess Arribel. Why have you come to our domain?"

"Lord Tartarus Kai. I have come to speak to you and your kind on an urgent request."

"How urgent is this request you have brought?"

"There was a man who was taken captive by my father. He escaped and fled. Most likely out in the desert. I have come to ask if you have seen this man."

Tartarus nodded, rubbing his chin. He shrugged shoulders without question. Just calm.

"I have not come across a Micran. Nor would one of them step foot near this forest by any means."

"As I told your guardsmen, this man is not a Micran. He's not from Argoron. He's from someplace else."

"Then, where did this prisoner originate from? The stars above? A planet far from our own?"

"Those are a possibility." Lola said. "I just need to find him before-"

"Before the Wyvern King has him, right?"

"Yes."

"Well, for all that it's worth, the Wyvern King probably has the prisoner by now. We have not seen this man anywhere near the forest."

Lola sighed with worry as Serai went to calm her. Tartarus stepped forward, looking down at the princess. He saw she had concern for the prisoner, which he deemed strange considering she didn't not fully know the origins or personality of the prisoner.

However, he saw that she could see what would come to pass if Porter had been taken by the Wyvern King and what he could be used for. Being the Wyvern King is an adversary to his own ruler ship, Tartarus laid his hand on Lola's shoulder.

"I have an offer for you."

"Which is?"

"Sense the prisoner did not come across this region and it is more than likely the Wyvern King has taken him to Alderan, I will lend you two of my warriors to accompany you in your search."

"Um, I'm not sure what to say to that."

"No need. The better the Wyvern King doesn't have an upper hand the better."

"And what will you do if my father discovers you helped me?"

"Then, I will have a share of words with your father. Respectfully. No need for Micrans to fight against Celedians while the Wyvern kind continue to roam above our heads like *turuls*."

Lola agreed as the two Celedians stepped onto her chariot and they rode off with Tartarus watching as he turned back and entered the forest.

Elsewhere, the Wyvern Men flew down over a city. The city was complete made of mud bricks, detailed in the sand of the desert. The wyvern men carried Porter as they entered into a huge kingdom, the kingdom of Alderan. Overseen by the Wyvern King. The city was surrounded by full-grown wyverns hovering and flying across the sky. Inside the kingdom, the others who dwelled there appeared to be part-human and part-wyvern themselves with only a slight few being completely humanlike or wyvern-like. They took Porter into the rock-layered palace. Inside, they set Porter on the ground and stood beside him. Porter remained unconsciousness as he was overseen by other wyvern men. Dressed in armor from their heads to their feet..

"Is this the man you saw, my king?" one of the wyvern men asked.

"Why yes." said the Wyvern King as he entered the palace. "This is the one who caught my eyes."

Porter's body jolted as he began to regain consciousness. Raising his head slowly, finding himself surrounded by wyvern men and standing before him, the Wyvern King. Porter raised up quickly, attempting to stand on his feet as the wyvern men rushed over, holding him down on his knees with their hands pressing against his shoulders.

"No need to worry, strange man." The Wyvern King said. "You'll soon get the answers you seek."

Porter stared at the Wyvern King as he sat down in his throne seat, sitting with one leg stretched out and a sinister grin on his face. His eyes piercing like a dragon and his claws sharp both on his hands and feet. His skin was rough and darker than the sands.. Porter staggered as he continued to try and stand up.

"Who are you?" Porter asked.

"I am your new lord and master, I am the Wyvern King."

"The Wyvern King. Where the hell am I?"

"You're in the city of Alderan. My domain of ruler-ship. Where else could you be?"

"I demand my exit. I demand to return home."

"Oh, you wish to return to Taranopolis?"

"Taranopolis? I'm not from this place. This planet. I want to return to Earth."

The Wyvern King paused, standing up from his seat, steeping down the stairs toward Porter. The King inched closer to get a better look at Porter. Seeing his skin, his hair, and his eyes. The wyvern King scoffed.

"You're telling me you're from the world beyond?"

"the world beyond? I'm from the planet called Earth."

"My lord," a wyvern men said. "I believe he speaks of the world of Jagoron."

"Jagoron. Ah, the place where the waters outnumber the land. You come from such a place?"

"I do and I wish to return there."

"Well, I'm not sure how you ended up here. But, I am most

definitely unsure how you'll return there."

"You cannot keep me here." Porter said. "I am not some prisoner."

"I beg to differ. The Wyvern King rebutted. "You see, when I saw you back in Taranopolis, the Micrans were bringing you in as their prisoner. In between then and now, you somehow made your escape and now, you're here in my city. In my kingdom. Therefore, you and now my prisoner and the only way those who are granted their leave from my kingdom is through combat."

"Combat?"

"If you can survive the Pit, you can have your freedom."

"I'm not a gladiator." Porter said. "I do not fight for sport!"

"You are one now. Survive my Pit. Entertain my guests and freedom will be yours."

The Wyvern King commanded his soldiers to take Porter to the dungeons. They stand Porter on his feet and Porter lunged toward the King with his fists, the King, using his own weight, pushed himself back as his wings emerged, taking up much of the space surrounding the throne. Terror had slithered into Porter as he eyes widen from the wingspan. The Wyvern King rushed toward Porter, punching him in the face. Porter fell to his knees from the sharpening blow.

"Take this specimen to the dungeons, now." the Wyvern King said.

"Yes, my king."

CHAPTER 6: TO WIN BATTLES IS TO WIN WARS

They drug Porter to the dungeons, throwing him in and shutting the doors. Porter rushed to his feet, taking a gander around the dungeon, seeing no one else inside with him. He approached the steel doors and gazed out, seeing a group of wyvern men standing and talking with one another. Unable to make out their conversation, he heard a thud against the wall on the opposite side of the dungeon. From there came muffled sounds of screams and beatings. The wyvern men turned back, looking toward the opposite dungeon and rushed over, opening the door. Porter could hear the wyvern men yelling and their wings flapping. Afterwards was only silence as the wyvern men stepped out from the dungeon, carrying a prisoner dressed in golden armor. Porter looked, seeing the prisoner appeared to be a human.

"What have you done to him?" Porter questioned.

"Quiet, slave. We do not answer to you."

"He's a human. You're keeping humans as slaves for what?"

"You ask why you're here? Because the audience needs entertainment. Today, is your attempt at giving it to them. By the orders of our king."

A loud horn roared across the sky. Porter gazed up and so did the two wyvern men. They looked to each other before turning toward Porter. One of them approached the door, unlocking it as the other entered the dungeon, fighting off Porter as they dragged him out and into another room. This room was full of other soldiers. Warriors from other lands outside of Alderan. Porter looked at them. Seeing the appeared to be human to his understanding. However, they only stared at him with confusion and strangeness. One of the gladiators stepped forward. A rugged-looking man. He stood over Porter by three feet. His stern demeanor proved he had been in Alderan for quite some time. Staring Porter in the eyes.

"The hell are you supposed to be?" He said, measuring Porter. "You're no Azurian."

"Get out of my face." Porter replied. "Before you end up on the ground."

"Or what? You'll kill me?" The gladiator chuckled. "Seeing as how we're all here to die anyway."

One of the wyvern men pointed toward Porter, demanding he remove his clothing. Porter disagreed, declaring he will keep on his uniform. The wyvern men rushed to him, stripping away his clothing. They left him naked as he looked around for something to cover himself with. One of the gladiators tossed him a tunic, which was detailed in its blood-red appearance with a golden sash. Porter put on the tunic as the wyvern men presented to him two golden leather gauntlets for his forearms. One of the gladiators tossed him a pair of boots with a leather-like appearance. However, when Porter touched them, the leather seemed unusual.

"What's this made of?"

"Enfield hide." the gladiator replied.

"Enfield?"

"They're very rare around these regions. Strong, brute creatures. You'll run in terror if you ever see them."

Porter nodded.

"I understand your concern."

Porter put on the boots when a wyvern man stood before him, holding a chest piece. He tossed it to Porter, commanding he put on he chest piece. Porter looked at the armor, feeling its ruggedness and its smoothness. Porter had asked if the armor had been previously used, only to receive the answer the armor belonged to a gladiator who was killed in battle several days prior. Porter looked at the center of the chest piece, noticing an insignia.

"What does this mean?"

"It means a stranger across worlds." The gladiator told him.

"Must mean the one who wore this came from another world." Porter said.

"He did. The place called Vanagon."

"Vanagon?"

"The second world from the distance of the Great Sun."

"Venus." Porter said quietly to himself.

Standing by the entry point of the armory and preparation room were two larger wyvern men. Both carried spears. They rallied the gladiators and Porter to prepare themselves for the fight ahead. Each of them formed an orderly line. Porter only looked on as they were searched and measured by the wyvern men. Seeing only their nods as the they were led toward the coliseum doors. The doors were over twenty-feet in height and the cheer of the crowd began to echo through them. Porter saw the gladiators were ready for the battle. Others were crying in fear. Porter kept himself calm as the gladiator he talked with stood beside him. Each of them were handed swords. Porter looked at the sword, seeing its sharpness and its light-weight.

"Strange material."

"Only found in the deepest parts of the Hibarian Forest."

"What's it made of?"

"Fallen star I was told. Possibly not."

"I see."

"Whatever you see out there, make sure not to give in to fear."

"What are you saying?" Porter questioned.

"What we're up against may seem terrifying to you. If you're like the others. For there are many beings and creatures which appear in these fights. All for the glory of sport."

"I'm not afraid. I just want to get out of here."

"Very well then. Survive the coliseum and you'll have it."

"I'm aware. Thanks for the tip. What is your name by the way?"

"Nakir. Yours?"

"Mark Porter."

One of the larger wyvern men stood by the door, glaring at the gladiators. He slammed the spear into the ground as the roar of the crowd soared behind him.

"Gladiators! Warriors of Alderan. This day, you will enter these gates and fight your way through a collage of beasts. A sea of soldiers from distant lands. I do not expect many of you to survive. For our king has gathered himself quite the nice spectacle for each of you to see. This fight will be one of the biggest ones Alderan has yet to put on and you all should be lucky to have participated within it. Now, I ask you. Do any of you seek your freedom? Then, if you do, you know what must be done. Survive and you'll have your freedom. Die and you'll have your freedom. If the gods permit it, of course."

The doors opened as the gladiators rushed out into the open field with only the sand of the grounds surrounding them. Porter and Nakir stood close as the other gladiators looked around at the crowd. Seeing the audience of a mixed-multitude. Porter was astonished by their presence.

"Didn't realize there were this many people living out here."

"Alderan is only a place for entertainment." Nakir said. "These people come from other lands. Distant from Taranopolis among others."

Porter looked straight ahead, seeing three other doors with wyvern men standing beside them. Porter pointed toward them as Nakir took notice.

"What's behind the doors?"

"The terror and dread which shall soon wash over the gladiators."

The Wyvern King walked out in the midst of the crowd, overseeing the grounds. Porter looked up, spotting him as he showered himself in the cheers. The Wyvern King sat down in a seat of his own. Similar to his throne. He raised his right hand toward the wyvern men at the first door. Signaling for it to open. They obeyed and the first door opened with all the gladiators prepared.

"Here we go." Nakir said.

Busting from the first door were tall, thin, and green looking creatures. Ten of them. They walked upright similar to humans, but they were not as they had shades of grass growing on their arms and legs and mushrooms on their shoulders, covered up by the armor around their torsos. No hair, long arms, legs, and their eyes were as white as snow. They roared together as they rushed toward the gladiators.

"The hell are they?" Porter wondered.

"Plant Men." Nakir answered. "Dwellers from the Hibarian Forest in the secluded lands."

"Noted."

The Plant Men collided with the gladiators. All fighting with swords. Some had shields which were scattered throughout the coliseum grounds. Porter saw one shield and ran over to grab it. Once he had it, a Plant Man dove over him with a sword and Porter blocked the attack with the shield and found an opening as he swiped the shield across the Plant Man's face and impaled him with the sword. Nakir battled a Plant Man, killing him by cutting off the legs and head. Porter looked round at the other gladiators, seeing them being overrun by the Plant Men. Porter couldn't take the sight as he intervened, crashing against the Plant Men with sword and shield. Nakir joined in and fought alongside him. So far, eight of the twenty prisoners were killed by the Plant Men. Porter and Nakir continued to fight as did the remaining prisoners. Inspired by Porter's relentlessness. Porter led the remaining gladiators against the last four Plant Men and they quickly decimated them with their swords. The Wyvern King stood up in awe and anger. His sight focused on Porter. He knew there was something to him and signaled for the second door to open, which came out were six-legged beasts. Two were hairless aside from the large manes around their necks. Four of them roaring and snarling. Porter stared as he saw hem walking out and the gladiators began to show signs of fear.

"Are those lions?" Porter asked.

"No." Nakir answered slowly. "Those are Beoths."

The Beoths roared in fury toward the gladiators. Mixing their ferocity with the cheers of the crowd. The gladiators banded together as the beoths charged toward them with their fangs and claws. One beoth leaped, lunging atop the gladiators as they held their shields overhead. Porter looked for an opening and slicked the back leg of the beoth as they shoved the large beast off the shields. A second beoth snatched one of the gladiators by his leg, dragging him and tossing him in the air as the others scattered around the area in sight of the beoths.

"Move with me!" Porter screamed.

The gladiators did not take heed to Porter's command as two beoths circled them. In front of Porter and Nikar jumped another beoth. Snarling as it stared into their eyes. Porter swiped the sword across the beast's face before kicking it in the nose. The beoth swiped with its pawed claws, scratching Porter in the leg. The beoth swiped again, knocking the shield to the ground. Nikar grabbed the shield as the beoth jumped over him. Nikar pressed against the beast's strength as it went for his head with its jaws. Porter saw Nikar on the ground and the beoth over him. He pressed on in pain from the scratch and leaped atop the beoth like a bull. The beast jumped around, trying to toss Porter from its back. Porter held his ground, raising the sword with one hand and impaling the beoth in its neck. One down as Porter helped Nikar to his feet.

"Thanks."

"No problem."

They looked on, seeing the gladiators stood no chance against the two circling them. They went to aid them before the other beoth jumped in front of them. This one more hairy than the last as Porter swiped the sword against it, but the hide and hair of the beoth was took thick for a strike. The beoth charged, slamming Porter into the arena walls as it chased Nikar. Porter stood up, rubbing his right shoulder, seeing the blood. He sighed as he made a run toward Nikar. Nikar dodged a paw swipe as Porter jumped on top of the beoth in similar fashion. The crowd savored all they were witnessing as did the Wyvern King. Porter held the sword, impaling the beoth in its neck, but the hair and hide were too durable.

"Dammit!" Porter shouted. "What are we going to do now?!"

Nikar stood, thinking. He looked over to the walls, seeing on the ground a long chain. Running over, he grabbed the chain and smelled it. Recognizing what material it was made of and he tossed it toward Porter. Porter caught the chain with his left hand as his right was occupied by the sword. The beoth leaped, tossing Porter from its back. Nikar ran toward Porter as the beoth charged at them both. Porter held the chain and told Nikar to stand back. Nikar moved as Porter stood up and wrapped the chain around the beoth's neck and pulled it back from the charge. The beoth's neck had snapped from the sudden strength of Porter, which startled Nikar and the crowd. Even the Wyvern King was intrigued. The beoth's body lumped into the sand as Porter looked at his hands and the chain.

"Where did that come from?"

"The other two!" Nikar yelled. "We need to finish them off!"

"Leave it to me." Porter answered. "Toss me the shield!"

Nikar grabbed the shield, tossing it toward Porter. He exhaled and ran toward the gladiators as they fought off the two beoths to a less result. Porter yelled for them to spread out and they followed his order. While the spread, they split up the two beasts, separating them from a distance. One was hairy and the other was hairless. Porter targeted the hairless one first by using the chain and pull its leg as he leaped over, stabbing it in the neck. Moving without haste, Porter used the chain to pull the final beoth, wrapping the chain around its neck and tossing it on its back. Porter looked,realizing the abdomen was not covered with hair nor was the skin thick. Porter jumped over the beoth and impaled the beast in its chest with the sword. The audience cheered as Porter whipped the chain back from the beoth's neck and stood in the middle of the area, looking at the audience. They began to applaud him. The other gladiators took notice and Nikar nodded.

"Ugh!" The Wyvern King said, standing up from his seat. "Give it up for Mark Porter!"

The audience cheered louder and chanted Porter's name. the Wyvern King grabbed a spear and threw it directly in front of Porter. Crashing into the sand within two feet of him. The Wyvern King pointed toward him and the other remaining gladiators.

"You have won this day. But, on the morrow, oh, it will be the day you shall die."

The Wyvern King swiped his hands as the wyvern men escorted Porter and the gladiators back to the dungeons. The night had settled and this time, Porter was kept in the dungeon with Nikar and the two spoke about their past before the arena. Nikar told Porter he had come from a place in the southern region of Argoron. A place he hoped to see again. Opening up, Porter began to tell Nikar of his home world of Earth. Nikar paused.

"You come from Jagoron?"

"I do. I guess Jagoron is your language for Earth."

"How did you get here?"

"I don't know. That's what I'm trying to find out."

"Once you achieve your freedom, I'm sure the answers will come."

"I hope so."

Elsewhere, Lola, Serai, and the Celedians took a stop at one of the Celedian camps several miles near Alderan. Lola looked ahead, seeing the city lights as the cold air blew over them. Serai handed Lola a cloak, one decorated in the royal redness of Argoron.

"We were informed of an event which happened in the city early this day."

"What did they say?" Lola asked.

"They said the audience was intrigued by a man. A strange one. He defeated beoths with ease. They said his strength was beyond comprehension."

Lola paused. Nodding to her own thoughts.

"It's him. It has to be."

"We'll find out in the morning. Right now, it is best you rest as shall we."

In the dungeon, Porter looked on, seeing Nikar was asleep. The area was silent. More silent than any place he's been since he had been on Argoron. He smirked, dreaming of his return to Earth and what he will tell those of his current adventure. He closed his eyes and fell into a deep sleep.

CHAPTER 7: FREEDOM OR SLAVERY

The next morning, the wyvern men bolted into the dungeons, awakening Porter, Nikar, and the gladiators. They prepared themselves and gathered their weapons which sat at the entry point of the arena. Porter listened as he heard the roaring crowd once again. The doors had opened and they went out. The Wyvern King stepped forward, commanding with a shouting voice that they open all three doors. The wyvern men obeyed as the doors opened. What Porter and the gladiators saw terrified them. From the first door entered a pack of wyverns. They flew toward the gladiators and they were prepared. Their hands gripped the hilts of their swords. Porter whipped his chain as he held the sword in his right hand. From the second door had arrived gladiators, however these were different. They were more brute in size and their skin glistened with the sunlight. Even their height towered Porter and the others.

"Those are the warriors from the faraway land." Nikar said.

"What's their stats?" Porter questioned.

"They kill whatever pleases them. Killing is only a sport for them."

"Noted." Porter nodded.

The brute gladiators ran toward them with force. While they were making their way near them, Porter looked ahead at the third door and he could feel the trembling in the ground. Looking at the sand, seeing it rise up and fall. Nikar could feel the tremors as well and he stepped back, leaving Porter in confusion.

"He has them." Nikar said. "He caught them."

"Has who?" Porter questioned. "Caught what?"

From the third door walked out two great and powerful creatures. Standing over thirty-five feet in height and incredibly hairy. One was as white as snow. The other was as dark as coal. The creatures smashed their arms in the ground, roaring to the cheer of the crowd. Porter stared at them. Impressed by their height and size.

"Are those gorillas?" Porter said.

"No." Nikar answered. "They are the Beasts of the wilderness. The white one is the Hoary Beast. While the black one is the Ruin Beast. Both are creatures of great destruction."

"We have to survive this."

"How?"

"Leave it to me." Porter said. "We're getting out of here this day."

The Beasts charged into the battle as the gladiators fought the brutes. The wyverns flew overhead, striking whenever they found an opening in the crowded swordfight. Porter gazed up toward a wyvern, using the chain to snatch the creature from the air to the ground. Once the wyvern had fell, Porter rushed over and impaled the creatures. He continued the same tactics to the other wyverns, only for one of the brute gladiators to tackle him to the ground. Porter rolled out of the path from the gladiator's large mace. Nikar ran into the fight, slashing his sword across the gladiator's arm, cutting it off with the mace in hand. Porter nodded to Nikar as he decapitated the brute. The wyverns continued with their snapping jaws, grabbing gladiators from the ground and throwing them across the arena, only for them to be stomped on by the Beasts. Porter took on two of the brutes with Nikar at his side. The gladiators who remained were quickly killed by the wyverns and Beasts. Leaving only Porter and Nikar to fight for themselves. Seeing themselves outnumbered. Porter focused his movement, striking the last two brutes with the chain and slashing the wyverns in the air as he jumped. Showing his impressive skill. Skills he didn't know he had before. Surprising the audience as Nikar stabbed the brutes after they were struck by Porter's chain. Several of the wyverns landed on the ground, seeking to lung on Porter. The wyverns went to pounce and the Beasts behind them trampled them without notice. Staring at Porter and Nikar as their prize.

"This is the day they die." The Wyvern King uttered.

Porter and the Hoary Beast come face-to-face. Porter jumped across the Beast to get a better shot with the sword, however the Beast took notice of the chain and snatched it, jerking Porter from the air, swinging him around until he is slammed into the sand as the Ruin Beast chases Nikar through the arena. Porter stood up, grabbing the chain with both hands, jerking it back towards him from the Hoary Beast. The Beast glared at Porter, huffing. The Hoary Beast slammed its fists into the sand, running toward Porter. Porter followed suit, charging toward the Hoary Beast himself with the sword in hand. Mark leaped into the air over the Beast's head, slashing the large creature down its back while landing a kick to the back of its head. The Beast stumbled from the slash and the kick fo only a few seconds as Porter landed on the ground. He turned around to face the Beast, twirling the chain. The Beast turned, staring at Porter. Porter grinned as he swung the chain with such force, it slapped the Beast in its head. The force of the chain whip caused the massive creature to fall and it laid in the sand with the audience in silence. Nikar looked over as he hid from the Ruin Beast in a corner, seeing the downed Hoary Beast. He smiled.

"He killed it!"

The Ruin Beast looked back, seeing the Hoary one dead. It roared with anger, preparing to charge toward Porter. Porter twirled the chain again, smirking. The Hoary Beast began to move slowly, attempting to raise itself up to its feet. Seeing the creature moving, Porter jumped on top of the creature's body and dug the sword through the throat, officially killing the creature. The Wyvern King glared with anger, yet signaled an applause for Porter's achievement. He began to clap and the audience followed suit. Porter turned to face the Wyvern King.

"I've taken down one of your Beast, Wyvern King." Porter yelled. "What more must I do to prove my freedom?!"

The Wyvern King raises his right arm as the wyvern men signaled the Ruin Beast's attention. Directing it toward Porter. The Beast roared and charged toward him. Porter paused for a moment, showing a faint sign of tiredness. Nikar stood up against the arena wall, cheering Porter on. He took notice and stood firm in the sand. Standing still in a fighting stance. Sword and chain both in his hands.

"Slaughter him!" The Wyvern King yelled.

The Ruin Beast looked down, seeing Nikar and proceeded to grab him from the wall. Porter ran over, pointing the sword toward the creature.

"Come at me!" Porter yelled toward the Ruin Beast. "Leave him alone!"

The Beast charged and once it reached closer, Porter jumped in the air, moving over the beast's head. He turned himself around in midair and raised the sword. The chain swiped against the creature's back and the sword itself was shoved through the back of its head, immediately killing it. The Wyvern King starts clapping and the audience begins clapping. Porter turns, facing the Wyvern King.

"I've taken down both your beasts, Wyvern King." Porter yelled. "What more must I do to prove my freedom is granted?!"

At the entrance to Alderan, Lola, Serai, and the Celedians arrive. Hearing the cheers of the crowd at the coliseum, they made haste toward it. Meanwhile, inside the arena, the Wyvern King stood up from his seat, walking down to the arena grounds to confront Porter. The audience was intrigued by their king's motives. Two wyvern men accompanied their king as he stepped foot on the sands drenched in the blood of his gladiators and creatures. The Wyvern King stood before Porter. Nikar sat back against one of the podiums attached to the arena walls.

"You seek your freedom." The Wyvern King asked.

"Yes. However, not only my own. But, his as well." Porter said, pointing toward Nikar.

The Wyvern King chuckled.

"I see. Very well. You have achieved your freedom. You are a free man. But, you have sought to gain the freedom of another. Therefore, there is one more fight you must endure."

Within the crowd, Lola, Serai, and the Celedians entered.

Looking ahead as they saw Porter standing face-to-face with the Wyvern King. Lola wanted to go down and save him, but the Celedians resisted. Demanding she wait and watch what might come. Unsure of their ideas, she hesitated her own hastiness and sat down to watch.

"And what must I endure?"

"A final battle."

"Against what?" Porter asked. "More gladiators? More beasts?"

"No. Against me"

The wyvern men handed their king a spear. He stretched forth his wings, showing them to the audience, only to hear their cheers as they screamed his name. he grinned at the sound as Porter stepped back, gripping the chain and sword. The wyvern men on the ground flew away. Leaving their king and Porter on the field. Nikar stepped forward, only for Porter to raise his hand toward him. Nikar stepped back, nodding.

"Are you ready to die?" The Wyvern King asked.

"I won't die today." Porter answered.

The Wyvern King quickly attacked with the spear and his long tail covered in spikes. Porter deflected the spear and tail with the sword. Porter swiped the chain across the Wyvern King's chest, only to hit the armor. The Wyvern King laughed as he used the spear to trip Porter. He stood over him, holding the spear and Porter moved himself out of the weapon's path and wrapped the chain around the Wyvern King's leg, pulling him to the ground. He went to impale the Wyvern King to the ground, but the wings pulled him back and the tail of the King swiped Porter across his chest, knocking him to the ground. The audience was back and forth in reactions to the two dueling.

"You won't win this." The Wyvern King said.

"Keep fighting and we'll see."

The spear was raised, only for Porter to slash the sword across it, snapping it in half. He grabbed the end of the spear and shoved it in the side of the Wyvern King, causing him to stumble in his steps. Through the pain, he continued to fight, pulling the spear from his ribs and throwing it to the sand. He punched Porter across his face several times before grabbing him by his throat and slamming him. He set his foot over Porter's chest, raising his spiked tail above him.

"Give up."

"I will never."

Porter swiped the sword, cutting the ankle of the King. He kicked him back and stood up, using the chain to swipe against eh armor as it began to break from the constant blows. Porter had the Wyvern King down on his knees as he ripped the chest piece from him and impaled the sword. Gasps filled the air as Porter stared into the Wyvern King reptilian eyes.

"I am… not dead yet."

"Don't be sure of yourself."

Porter removed the sword and decapitated the Wyvern King. His body collapsed to the ground and the wyvern men around the arena let out a screeching yell. A yell in pain and agony. It was there, the Celedians busted into the arena, killing any wyvern men that did not fly away. At the entrance entered Tartarus Kai. He looked out at the audience and glanced down at the dead body of the Wyvern King.

"Citizens of Alderan! The tyrant is now dead! From this day forward, Alderan belongs to the Celedians!"

Porter approached Tartarus and nodded, holding the chain and sword.

"I think I'll be keeping these."

"Suit yourself. But, you have visitors who are expecting you."

Tartarus pointed toward the arena gates, seeing Lola standing. Porter looked at her and was unsure, yet, her beauty caught his gaze. Something he was not familiar with on this planet. Otherwise, Porter nodded to Nikar. Their freedoms were won as they exited the arena with the crowd cheering around them. In front, Lola approached them both, but her eyes were set on Porter.

CHAPTER 2: A HERO?

"I am Princess Lola Arribel of Taranopolis and I've been searching for you." Lola said.

"Ok, Princess." Porter replied. "Why, madam have you been searching for me?"

"Because you're needed. I saw you fight. Your skills. Your strength. You have what it takes to save us. To possibly save us all."

"I'm needed? Needed for what?"

"To help us stop what's coming."

"And what is coming?" Porter questioned.

"Her father, King R'akl has been betrayed by Saban Jai." Tartarus said.

Lola looked toward him, questioning how he would know of such information. Tartarus informed her that he set spies throughout Taranopolis and many of them received information of Saban's betrayal after making an alliance with the Wyvern King. Tartarus described the plans of Saban's intentions to have been revealed after he married Lola. Striking them at a most vulnerable position.

"Mr. Porter." Lola said, standing in front of him. "I need your help in this matter. Please, help my father and his people from Saban's betrayal."

"Porter looked down, nodded and gazed the surroundings. He shook his head in decline.

"I'm sorry. I just want to go home."

"Home?"

"Yes. Home. I'm not from this planet. Your political matters do not concern me."

"But, you're here on Argoron. Yet, there is something strange about you. You don't have the complexion to be an Argoronian."

"Of course not. I'm from Earth."

"Jagoron? Wait, how can you be from a world beyond ours?"

"I'm not sure myself. I seek to return there. I need to know how."

"I know of a way." Tartarus said.

"What is it?" Porter questioned. "Whatever it is you are."

"I am a Celedian. King of my kind. The name is Tartarus Kai."

"Mark Porter. Of Earth. Now, tell me what you know? How can I return home?"

"There is a portal caught in the rift of a pillar. A strong one."

"Where is this pillar?"

"Between the borders of Taranopolis and Alderan. If you take one of the travellers, you can make it there before nightfall."

"And if I go on foot?"

"Then, you'll be trekking in the dune sands for several days. Two at most."

Porter agreed to the offer as one of the Celedian warriors had presented him a traveller. Porter scoffed as he saw the vehicle. He walked around it, measuring it out.

"No tires?" Porter said.

"Tires?" Tartarus asked. "What is that?"

"They go on the bottom. Four on each side."

"This traveller needs no bottom compartments. Once you're inside, the controls will tell you what you must do."

"And how does it travel?"

"Anti-gravity."

"Interesting."

Porter entered the traveller as it powered up. The gear was in place and Porter was prepared to leave. Tartarus asked if Porter wanted a test run of the vehicle, yet Porter denied the request, preferring to learn as he goes. Tartarus understood and stepped back. Lola rushed toward the traveller, placing her hands on the door.

"You cannot just go along and leave us to a possible destruction."

"Look, madam. I'm sorry for what is happening in your home.

But, I'm not from here. I'm just a foreigner and I want to return home."

"And will your conscience be content with your decision?"

Porter sighed. He gave Lola a stare.

"We'll see."

The traveller roared as it levitated over the ground. Porter jerked the wheel as he glared down at the ground, seeing the sand blow around the vehicle. Porter nodded to Tartarus and Lola as he rode away. Lola sighed in slight anger as Tartarus approached her.

"Don't worry yourself. There is a reason why myself and my warriors are here."

"What do you mean?"

"We cannot allow you and Serai to return to Taranopolis only to fall in Saban's hands. We'll accompany you and protect you and your father from Saban's army."

"And I guess you'll want my father to grant you something in return?"

"We'll talk about that after Saban is dealt with."

Lola agreed to Tartarus' assistance as he rallied all the Celedian warriors and they rode off toward Taranopolis.

CHAPTER 9: THE EARTHMAN'S CHOICE

Mark Porter rode out into the desert, gazing up toward the sun as he took note of its slow descending. He continued to ride and far out in the distance, Porter saw something standing in the middle of the sands. Coming up onto the object closer, Porter knew it was the pillar. Standing over twenty feet and carved out of what may have been a small mountain in the area. Porter reached the pillar and exited the traveller.

"What kind of structure is this?"

Porter looked around the pillar, finding a small pond and several small trees growing around it. From the pillar itself fell a waterfall. Porter wasn't sure how such an object or environment operate in the middle of the desert. Porter approached the waterfall and began hearing faint sounds of voices. The voices were familiar to him. Familiar to the point the began to call out names.

"General?"

Back at Taranopolis, Lola and Serai had made their return with Tartarus and the Celedian warriors behind them. Entering the city and startling the people, Lola made haste toward the palace and she entered just as her father was speaking with Saban. She stooped herself in her steps with Serai by her side as they turned to see her. R'akl stood up from his throne and approached her as she knelt down. Saban was confused by her sudden appearance.

"We've been searching for you, my daughter."

"I'm sorry, father. But, I had to go out and find the prisoner."

"And did you?"

"Yes. He was in Alderan."

"Alderan." R'akl replied. "I knew it. I knew the Wyvern King would've taken him. He disobeyed my orders to keep him here. When I speak with him again, I will have much words for him."

"Father, the Wyvern King is dead."

Saban jolted and stepped forward with concern. R'akl only shook his head in hearing the words of the Wyvern Kong's death.

"What do you mean dead?" Saban questioned. "How do you know of this?"

"My daughter, who slew the Wyvern King of Alderan?"

"The prisoner. He called himself Mark Porter of Earth."

"Him." Saban said. "So, an earthman chooses to thwart Argoronian laws."

"You cannot blame him, Saban. He doesn't know our rules. How else could he have abided by them."

"We need to find this prisoner, my king. Before he comes here and tries to do the same to you. To me. To your daughter even."

"He had no intensions on killing me." Lola said.

"As of this moment." Saban replied. "My king, allow me and my warriors to go out into the dunes and find him. Bring him back and then, we can be rid of him."

Lola sighed, gathering their attention.

"There is something else, father. Something you must know."

"Speak it."

"The Celedians are here in he city."

"Celedians?!" Saban yelled. "Those savages!"

"Why are they here? And under who's orders did they receive permission?"

"They came to accompany me."

"Accompany you for what?"

"To protect you, father."

"Protect me?" R'akl replied with confusion. "Protect me from what?"

"Him." Lola said, pointing toward Saban.

R'akl turned toward Saban and they both gave looks of uncertainty. Layered with confusion. R'akl turned back to his daughter as Saban stood still, his eyes looking around the throne room.

"What proof do you have of this?"

Lola turned around as Tartarus Kai entered the throne room, ducking his head as he entered. Saban raised up his sword as he eyes widen toward the tall king. R'akl stood his ground, with his hand gently on the hilt of his blade. Tartarus stood before them both, yet, bowed his head before R'akl.

"King of Taranopolis. I did not come to make war."

"Why are you here, savage king?" Saban asked.

R'akl raised his hand, silencing Saban.

"Why have you accompanied my daughter back to her home?"

"I've placed several Celedian spies across your city for several months, king. I also had spies centered around Alderan and what they have informed me of, you must truly know. For it concerns the life of your daughter, your own, and your people."

"And what is this information?"

"Saban Jai is a traitor and a deceiver. He's been making plans alongside the Wyvern King to bring forth your demise. I told you daughter of this news and she has agreed to return here to tell you herself."

R'akl turned toward Saban. His eyes already speaking the truth.

"Why?" R'akl asked. "Why would you betray me? Betray all of us?"

Saban sighed, sheathing his sword and shrugging his shoulders.

"Because, it is time for all of Argoron to enter a new ruler-ship of power and might. In truth, my king, your rule has become weak. You grafted peace with this savage king and from there, you have only grown weaker. I knew it was the truth when the earthman appeared in the sands. There is other life out there. Other worlds in need of us. We have enough power to invade those planets and conquer them. Make them bow under Argoron laws and to worship our gods. Yet, you refuse. You want peace and nothing else."

"So, you sought to marry my daughter only to bring forth your plans of conquest?"

"I did. I have no reason to lie."

"It was never about love?"

"My king, it never was. Besides, you daughter is a beautiful woman. But, her hastiness and attitude can make even the best of men fall to their demise. I would not become one of them."

"Father, you know what must be done."

R'akl nodded.

"Saban Jai, I hereby place you under arrest."

Two Micran guards entered the room and stood beside Saban. R'akl commanded them to take Saban to the cell, but they refuse. Removing their helmets and presenting themselves as Warriors to Saban's cause. They raised up their swords and wetn to strike R'akl. Tartarus intervened and deflected the blows with two swords of his own. Saban ran out of the throne room as Serai moved beside Lola as they went and stood by her father as Tartarus commanded them both to leave and find safety.

Outside, the city is quickly placed under lockdown by Saban's warriors. In the streets stood Celedians and Micrans. Both on opposite sides as the Taranopolis civilians ran into their homes and evacuated themselves from the streets and open roads. Lola, Serai, and her father ran into one of the king's studies and locked the doors. At the palace, Saban stood at the balcony, overlooking the city and seeing his armies on the streets confronting the Celedians with their swords and spears. He grinned at the sight of it. Change appeared imminent.

"This day will prove that I am the new king of Argoron. The conquest is nigh."

In the desert, Porter continued to hear the voices coming through the waterfall. He slowly placed his hand in the water, feeling its coolness. Behind the waterfall seemed to be a cavern. From there, Porter placed his head through the waterfall and what he saw inside the cavern was a bright, spherical light.

"A wormhole."

He stepped into the cavern and approached the wormhole. Gazing inside, Porter began to make out an image. Looking closer as the seconds passed. Porter saw within the wormhole was a facility. Still looking, he recognized several vehicles parked. Porter's eyes widen.

"Area 51. Earth."

Seeing he was standing at the door, Porter took one step forth and-

CHAPTER 10: THIS IS ARGORON

Taranopolis is set between two forces as its civilians have fled into their homes and other nearby buildings. All in the fear of what's before their eyes. In the streets of the city, the Micrans and Celedians stood facing one another. Each of them wielding swords, spears, staves, and maces. Micrans even held shields as they stepped in the front of the face-off. Saban remained on the balcony, overseeing the two armies.

"This day, my warriors will overcome these savages and the city will thank me. Everyone will thank me."

Saban grabbed a bow and arrow from the table and set the arrow into one of the firepots on the balcony. He aimed smoothly and fired a shot into the middle of the armies. They saw the arrow pierce into the sand. The Micrans gazed up to the balcony, seeing Saban. From there, they yelled and charged toward the Celedians with force. Seeing the Micrans coming, the Celedians rallied themselves and ran into the fight with both forces colliding with weapons and shields.

Meanwhile as the battle commenced, R'akl remained inside the study with Lola and Serai. He hung his head, sulking in the shame of having such favor in Saban, only to have been betrayed. Lola informed her father that all will be well and once Saban is gone, they can continue on in life. R'akl took note of his daughters' words and yet, he continued to say that a king must rule Argoron. It is the natural law of the planet and the balance of their faith. Lola did not argue. She understood everything well. From the doors bolted in

Tartarus, calming them down from his sudden appearance.

"Where is Saban?" R'akl asked.

"I do not know." Tartarus answered. "He fled from the throne room as soon as the fighting began."

"He's still here." Lola said. "He wouldn't have fled the city. He wants to look like the victor once the fighting has ceased."

"Then we must find him." Tartarus said.

"Go." R;akl said. "find Saban and bring him to me. He will face a swift justice."

"And what if he refuses to come alive?" Lola asked.

R'akl sighed and waved his hand. Lola nodded, looking back to Tartarus. The Celedian king understood the king's answer without a word and left the study.

On the streets, the Micrans and Celedians are slaughtering each other. Spears impaling, swords slashing, and shields deflecting. Some Micran warriors jointed into units of two and ambushed several Celedians who's heights exceeded even the average ones. Saban continued to watch as Tartarus searched for him throughout the palace. Lola sat with Serai and whispered something in her ear as she stood up and went for the door.

"Where are you going?" R;akl asked.

"To find Saban."

"Without someone to accompany you?"

"Tartarus is out there. I'm sure he'll be with me."

"Watch yourself out there."

Lola nodded with a smile as she headed out for Saban.

Saban grabbed a chair and sat down, overseeing on the ongoing slaughter. He smirked, eating fruit and drinking wine. Standing behind him were two servants. Servants he rallied from within the city and stand with him as they watch the battle. Saban promised them greater positions under his rule. Bolting into the balcony behind was Tartarus with his sword drawn. Saban jumped up in a surprise fashion.

"Who let a savage into the upper floors?!"

"Only a fool would seem to find you on the streets in battle. Yet, you choose to watch like a worthless king."

"I am a king! Look down there! Your warriors are falling to mine. This day, you shall bow before me!"

"Oh no, betrayer. My warriors are known to overcome any amount of forces that appear before them. Your warriors will disobey your commands. For you are not their king."

Saban paused himself, his eyes glanced down toward the edge of the balcony where his sword rested. He jumped for the sword as Tartarus slammed his sword down, breaking the furniture as Saban slid on the marbled floor, grabbing his sword. He raised it up just as Tartarus' own clashed with it. The servants left the balcony and Saban grinned.

"A fight you want?"

"How else can your warriors see you for the false king you truly are."

Saban yelled, jumping on his feet and swinging his sword. He and Tartarus fought on the balcony as the fighting in the streets continued. Lola walked through the palace in search for Saban. She arrived outside, seeing the fighting in front of her. Blood spilling from the dead warriors. One of the Micrans ran toward her, beaten and bloodied. The warrior begged to hear word from her father. She had no reply as he warrior returned into battle. Hearing the clashing of weapons. She noticed the sound of clashing coming form above. Stepping out on the steps, Lola glared up to see Tartarus and Saban fighting.

"Oh no."

She moved with speed to reach the balcony as they continued fighting. Saban gained the upper hand on Tartarus by tripping him and he hanged on the edge. Saban grinned.

"Let's see if a Celedian can survive such a fall."

Tartarus went for a swipe, only to be kicked by Saban off the balcony, breaking the edge. The armies paused as Tartarus fell to the ground. Saban looked down at Tartarus' body. He smiled and made his way down, using a rope attached to his waist armor. Tartarus was still breathing, only in pain. Saban cocked his head, placing his foot over the Celedian King's body and looking out at both armies.

"I am your king now!"

The Micrans paused themselves in confusion. Seeing Saban wielding the sword in the air. The Celedians were more concern with their king's condition. Lola had made it to the balcony, only to see the broken edge and both Tartarus and Saban on the ground. Saban commanded both armies to bow before him and neither obeyed. Sensing their opposition, he yelled again, commanding them to bow. They did not bow.

"I am your king! King of Taranopolis! King of Argoron. My marriage to Princess Lola Arribel makes me your king!"

"Yet, we are not married yet." Lola said from above.

Saban turned around, gazing up. He grinned.

"Ah. The feat I have accomplish this day grants us our marriage and my ruler-ship as king. Who else could have taken out the Celedian king. The king of savages!"

"Did you kill him?" Lola asked.

"He's barely dead. Little close I'm afraid."

"You'll pay for this."

"By who's hand? Your father's?"

"No." A voice replied from the streets.

Saban looked out as did the armies. Lola saw who was standing and a large smile formed upon her face. Tartarus' eyes looked up to see and he was pleased. Saban stepped off of Tartarus' body to confront him. Porter had returned.

"You come here uninvited?'

"I am." Porter said.

Saban chuckled, stepping down the stairs to face Porter. He looked him in the eyes and scoffed, backing up in his steps and raising up his sword.

"You think you can defeat me?"

"I know I can."

"That right?"

"Yes."

Porter raised up his sword and whipped the chain. Saban saw the chain and rubbed his chin. Impressed with Porter's choice of weaponry.

"Must be a Jagoron skill."

"You'll find out."

Saban screamed as he charged toward Porter with his sword. Porter deflected the attack and whipped the chain across Saban's back, cracking the armor. Saban paused, trying to look back at the armor. Porter nodded as Saban ripped the armor from his torso.

"I do not need the armor to defeat you."

Saban swung the sword several times, hitting Porter's own with Porter kicking Saban in the knee and tripping him on the sand. Porter yelled for Saban to stand up and continue fighting. Saban flipped himself up and ran after Porter. From there, Porter used the chain and grab Saban's sword. Snatching it from his hand and slicing his chest. Saban fell back as Porter stood over him with the sword in front.

"Do you yield?"

Saban chuckled, wiping the blood from his face.

"I'm not finished here. I am king."

"You are NOT King!" said R'akl standing behind him.

The Micrans saw him and instantly bowed before him. The Celedians had already went over and aided their king. Lola turned to her father before looking out at Porter and Saban.

"Stand back." R'akl said.

Porter nodded, stepping back from Saban as he stood up and turned to face R'akl.

"You have betrayed me, Saban Jai and I will not tolerate it."

"King R'akl, I was to marry your daughter. I was to be king."

"No. You are not king and you will no longer marry my daughter."

"This is not how Micrans do business!" Saban yelled. "You're disobeyed ancient Argoronian laws by this decision."

"I am king. Seems you have forgotten."

Saban looked out at the Micrans, seeing them bowed before R'akl. He looked around at everyone as anger brewed within him. Turning back to R'akl in anger. He had enough.

"I will not tolerate this any-"

R'akl took the staff he carried and swung it across Saban's head, breaking his neck. Saban's body fell into the sand and R'akl stood tall.

"A swift justice is done."

Lola approached Porter, amazed by his return.

"You thought I was leaving?"

"I did and how come you chose not to?"

"There's something here. Something calling to me. I'm not sure as to what it is. But, this planet, it needs my help. My world will heal itself. This one needs help now."

R;akl approached Porter, measuring him and looking at his daughter. He nodded with a smile.

"The decision is done." R'akl said.

"What decision?" Porter asked, looking over to Lola, who's smiling.

"For the protection of this kingdom and this planet, you will marry my daughter."

Porter nodded. Looking over to Lola. R'akl held out the staff and Porter placed both hands upon it. Lola had done the same. It was at that moment the two were married. The Micrans stood up and applauded them as the civilians came out of their homes to see the two. The bodies on the streets were cleared out and a ceremony was set the following day for Porter and Lola. He two had married just as Tartarus and R'akl came to an understanding. Tartarus left with the Celedians as Porter and Lola spent their honeymoon together.

During the night of the honeymoon while Lola slept, Porter was awake and walked out onto the rebuilt balcony, overseeing the city of Taranopolis. He smiled. Turning back to go inside, a voice called to Porter from the balcony. A strange one. Porter turned back to find himself facing an entity. Made of complete light. A bright white light. The light even had arms, legs, and a head.

"What are you?" Porter asked.

"I've been watching you since you arrived."

"Watching me? For what purpose?"

"A greater kind of purpose."

"And you are?"

"I… am a God of Argoron."

RAIDERS OF VANOK

CHAPTER 1: VANCE HARLAN

As astrologists and astronomers continued their research pertaining to other living beings throughout the universe, Vance Harlan, a man specialized in the scientific community of interstellar space proposed a plan. His plans to travel into the stars through a wormhole, hoping to come out into another galaxy filled with life. Vance pleaded his plans and works to many other scientists. All of whom rejected. Vance even went as far as to proceed with funding from his own ship to travel into space. Backers were not impressed. Stating Vance was living in a fantasyland hoping to collude with alien beings.

During one meeting with the Department of Defense, Vance entered the room, brushing his blonde hair before seeing it was cornered by guards. He nodded with cockiness as he was unimpressed by their sheer attempt of intimidation. Vance stepped forward, sitting down at the desk with four members of the Department.

"I see you have my files." Vance said, seeing an open folder. "Well, did you read it? Or glance through it?"

"Mr. Harlan, we went over your works. Every bit of it."

"Every bit. Including the footnotes regarding the amount of energy needed to supply such a travel?"

The Officials sat still, and Vance nodded slowly.

"I guess you did. Now I'm impressed."

"What we decided is that we cannot give you the funding for such a proposal."

"Why not? You read the file. You saw the details of this kind of mission. You know it's possible."

"Yes. We do." The second official said. "However, events prior to this mission have reverted our attentions elsewhere."

"Elsewhere? Like what the oceans?"

"This talk of alien life has gotten the public too far into our affairs and we, don't like that fact."

"But, come on. It's aliens. An opportunity to speak with intelligent life outside of our own planet."

"We hear you."

"But?' Vance said with a quick sigh of breath.

"We're invested in or current public affairs. The funding must go there."

"I don't agree with this."

"Doesn't matter if you do or do not." The third official said. "The decision has been made regardless of your work."

Vance wiped his face and slanted his head. He clapped his hands, startling the officials and jolting the guards. Vance looked around at he guards, seeing their firearms slightly raised. He waved them off with a laugh.

"Even they get startled."

"Thank you for your time with us, Mr. Harlan. You may go."

"I do however have one question to ask you. Just one."

"What is it?" The first official said.

"What is the true reason you have denied me funding for this project?"

The first official sighed before gazing over to the other three. The second official shook his head, staying silent. The third official fanned his hands in the air and didn't give an answer. The fourth official stared at Vance and turned to the first official. Giving him a nod. Vance's eyes moved back and forth between the for officials.

"So, is he going to tell me or are you? I'm confused right now with all this staring and waving."

"I will speak it for you." The fourth official said.

"Good." Vance replied. "That's good. Now, what is it?"

"There was an incident that occurred over a month ago in Nevada."

"Nevada. Ok. I'm still not getting at what you're trying to tell me."

"An incident of forceful attacks took place at Area 51. One of our lieutenants went missing in the light of fire after the base was ambushed. He was unable to be found and is still missing."

"I see. But, with all due respect, what does a missing lieutenant have to do with my project's funding?"

"The cause of the attack were those intelligent beings you're so amazed by. They ambushed the base and attacked our men. Killed many and one of our best lieutenants is nowhere to be found. Now, do you understand why we cannot permit this project to go forward? Because those things you desire to meet, they want us all dead and this world theirs."

"Well, maybe they were antagonistic aliens. I mean all aliens cannot be enemies, sir. That's just not possible."

"Either way. This project is not going forward. You may leave us now, Mr. Harlan. Return to your other work. It's proven useful for our country and your life."

Vance stood up from the desk, grabbing his file. He still continued speaking with the officials, pleading they give him the funding. The officials continued to refuse until the guards stepped down from their post and surrounded Vance. Fully realizing his current predicament, Vance nodded and chuckled before taking his leave. Vance had returned to his home and from here, he set for to find a way to get his project going without the funding from the Department. Working nonstop for months while living in the outskirts of Phoenix, Arizona looking for an opportunity, Vance had come into communication with a much-wealthy foreign billionaire. The billionaire did not give Vance his name or location, only that he was interested in Vance's work and handed him the funding he needed. The billionaire's only request was for Vance to return to

Earth once he had come into contact with extraterrestrials and that he should bring back with him physical evidence of their existence. Vance agreed to the commands and went ahead with the project. From there, a starship was built under the eyes of his colleagues and associates. Vance kept the project's workings to himself to avoid scrutiny and possible arrest from the government.

"Ah." Vance said, gazing at the starship. "She is finished."

The starship sat inside one of the hangars Vance had acquired from the military due to his previous works. Everything was in place for the travel and Vance had decided to wait until one clear night had come to make his launch. A week had passed and there was no clear sky due to the amount of clouds and precipitations of rainfall. Vance was annoyed by the weather's behavior. As if it was acting aggressive toward him, trying to get him to quit his project. Vance didn't quit and after a long day of rain, the night had come and the sky was clear. Vance had gathered all his gear and placed it inside the starship. The hangar had opened and the starship had launched into the sky. Vance was astonished at the speed of the ship and the stars around him. Several minutes had passed before Vance found himself in space, glancing out of the window looking down at Earth. Using a map he had placed inside the ship to navigate his goings. He went ahead and traveled. Passing through a stream of asteroids, a flash of light peaked through them, gaining Vance's attention. He moved toward through the meters toward the moving light. Once he came closer, the light flashed with such brightness that it caused the ship to jolt and from there, Vance could feel himself being pulled into the light and the ship with him. Vance kept his eyes shut from the blinding white-then-blue-then-red light. In a short spot of chance, Vance took a peek and saw the light was in fact a wormhole. A smile had formed on his face as he and the ship were sucked in and the light was gone. As if it was nowhere to be found. Like it was never in the stream of asteroids.

Within seconds, the ship was forced out of the wormhole with such speed, the ship had crashed onto a planet. Vance was calm, yet angry of his ship's damage. Exiting the damaged ship. Vance looked around, realizing he could breathe in the air. He looked down, seeing soil and grass. He grabbed the dirt and looked closer. It appeared to be no different than the soil on Earth.

"Shit!" Vance said. "Crashed back down to Earth."

While sighing in anger, the sound of a rushing wave crashed behind him. Vance had turned, looking at what he cold tell was a shoreline and the waves were crashing in with such force the ground had not flooded. Confused, he took a glance up to the sky and noticed it was a strange color. Not like the blue sky of Earth, but a very light greenish sky mixed with a layer of blue.

"What the hell?"

Vance had turned around to find himself quickly surrounded by beings that appeared to be hybrids. They had the upper bodies of animals and lower bodies of humans. They held what Vance could perceived to be guns toward him as he held his arms up. Somewhat shaking in fear. Not from the guns. One of the hybrids that appeared to be a Leopard-Man stepped forward, measuring Vance. He nodded.

"Take him back to the ship!"

"Ship?!" Vance said. "What ship?!"

CHAPTER 2: WELCOME ABOARD

Tossed onto a ship decorated with skulls of various creatures. Creatures unknown to Vance's knowledge, the ship took off across the waters as the crew passed him by, operating the ship's movement. Vance sat confused. Mainly confused by the living hybrids passing him by. Standing up, he wandered around the ship, attempting to ask questions concerning where he is. Turning around as the sea's waters rush against the ship, tilting it back and forth, Vance approached an somewhat middle-aged man dressed in Captain's garbs.

"Pardon me, but, where am I?"

"Where are you? My good sir, you aren't aware of your current circumstances?"

"What circumstances must I be aware of?"

"We found you on that small island. Looked to me, you must've crashed from the sea above us. We found you stranded out here. Brought you onboard to keep you alive. You do want to remain alive, don't you?"

"Well, yes I do. But, I'm not understanding. Where am I?"

"Where were you going?"

"I was going through a wormhole and I fell back down. I must be somewhere around the Pacific Islands. I have to be."

"Pacific Islands? What is that?"

Vance paused, looking at the Captain with uncertainty. He nodded while waving his hands, taking a gaze out toward the ocean.

"I'm still not understanding." The Captain said.

"We're on the Pacific Ocean, aren't we?"

"You're on the Sea of Aphro. The land around you is the Land of

Aphro."

"Aphro?" Vance said. "What is Aphro?"

The Captain led Vance toward his study within the ship, passing by more hybrid creatures working. They enter the study with the first thing Vance noticed were the amount of scrolls laying on the shelves and the desk. The Captain approached his desk and opened a drawer, searching through, he grabbed a scroll and signaled Vance to approach the desk. Vance stepped forward as the Captain opened the scroll.

"What is this?" Vance asked.

"A map of this planet. Where we are right now is in the District of Aphro. Riding over the Seas of course."

"Planet? You said planet?"

"I did. Yes."

"Hold on. So, you're telling me, we're not on Earth?"

"Earth?" The Captain said confusingly. "What is Earth?"

"Earth. You know the third planet from the sun."

"Third planet? Third planet… Oh, you speak about Jarok. You're from Jarok?"

"Jarok? No. I'm from Earth."

"But, you said third from the sun."

"That is Earth."

"It is where you're from. Here, it's pronounced Jarok. Other words have been thrown out before. Depending on what planet you land on."

"So, if this is not Earth, then where am I?'

"Vanok."

"What is Vanok?"

"The second planet from the sun. second before Jarok and second after Firoh."

"Firoh? Jarok? I'm not understanding these terms completely. You mean Earth and Mercury?"

"If that's what they're called wherever you're from?" The Captain replied. "So, you are from Jarok. Tell me, how are things there? We never receive news regarding that planet. Only the other ones around it."

Vance took a moment to catch his breath. Taking all of the information in slowly. If possible. He glanced down at the map, seeing the landmarks. What Vance noticed quickly was the amount of water upon Vanok and the mid-to-small sized islands surrounding two larger continents. He pointed at the continents with questions. What were they and who dwelled upon them. Asking the Captain concerning the two continents. The Captain chuckled, using a cane to point toward the continents.

"The one we're nearby, Aphro. Of course. The other is Vetor. Now, there is a difference between the two."

"What kind of difference?"

"Well, for starters, Aphro is a continent filled with rugged structures and a plethora of diverse creatures. That's where my hybrid pirates come in."

"A whole continent filled with beasts."

"Yes. Now, Vetor. It's a much different place. Surrounded by beautiful landmarks and cathedrals. From tall skyscrapers to temples to the Vanokian gods. Vetor is the home of the Kingdom of Vetoria."

"And have you ever been there? To this kingdom?"

The Captain laughed, taking a breath before walking over toward his shelf, where a bottle of rum sat. Grabbing the bottle and taking a drink.

"Never. My kind, meaning my line of work isn't seen as acceptable in such a place. The people of the kingdom perceive myself and those like me as subservient. Lesser living beings. The kingdom believes they're above all life on Vanok. Even their own children to an extent."

Vance remained quiet as the Captain took a moment of silence. He sighed and returned to drinking the rum as the ship rocked. Strangely enough, Vance felt the movement of the ship a bit strange. The ship rocked once more with the sound of a bang following. He stood up from his seat, looking around.

"Did you hear that?"

"Hear what?" The Captain asked.

"The explosion. Something's happening."

"Let's find out."

The two run out to the front, seeing the pirates clashing against another set of pirates as the opposing ship crashed into their own. From the other ship jumped over pirates of a different kind. Wearing worn-and-torn clothing with a particular circular insignia layered on their chest. Vance kept his distance as the Captain yelled for his pirates to assemble and fight against the others. Vance watched on as the swords clashed and the gunfire rung. In the distance on the other ship, Vance spotted a figure making themselves known. Looking closer, he saw the figure in full form.

"A woman?"

The woman stepped onboard the Captain's ship and fought against several of his hybrid pirates with a cutlass of her own. She took them down in seconds as she made her way toward the Captain. Vance sought to help, grabbing a sword on the floor and rushing toward the woman. Seeing him from the corner of her eye, she turned with speed clashing her cutlass against Vance's sword. She glared into his eyes and showed a slight grin.

"You're different." She uttered. "This is the ship."

The woman signaled her pirates to grab Vance and they tossed him onto the other ship as the Captain looked on fighting against the invaders. Making the move to assist Vance, he was slashed in the back by one of the pirates before the woman rallied her own to return to their ship. They moved with motion, returning to the ship and they escaped the area. The Captain stood up, sighing in pain went around to check on his pirates. Seeing some of them dead on the deck, he sighed bitterly.

"Her." He whispered to himself.

CHAPTER 3: CALYPSO

Vance had sat on the deck of the opposing ship, surrounded by the invading pirates. Their eyes eluded him. Glowing in many glares of color. From black, brown, green, blue, and red. The pirates snarled at Vance, attempting to terrify him. Yet, Vance kept his composure and faced them. The pirates from that point had paused themselves and moved over to the edges of the ship, making way for their captain to step forward. She walked with a vigorous stature as her eyes were set only on Vance. She approached him and looked down onto him. A grin had formed on her face.

"What's going on?" Vance asked. "Why did you take me?"

"Poor one. You aren't aware of the workings here. I can sense you're not from this world."

"Of course not. I come from Earth. As I was telling the Captain on the ship."

"You mean the Captain of those degenerate pirates?! Ha! Such company will poison you. Eventually killing you."

"Then, why take me from them? I was seeming to be doing just fine. Doing well for the most part since I crashed on this planet. What is all of this and where are you taking me?"

"Hold your temper and follow me."

The pirates escorted Vance behind the woman into her study. Looking similar to the Captain's own, yet detailed with colorful marbled walls and a stone-layered floor. Vance saw the floor and took a look back out to the deck, looking at its wooden bottom. He had questions and the woman only replied with the notion of her ship's design was possible due to her line of work. Vance wondered what work she spoke of as she sat down at her desk, covered with books and maps. Even a small emerald sat on the desk in the right corner. Like a pedestal of her achievements.

"Leave us." She told her pirates.

Exiting the study, Vance stood in the center of the room with the woman signaling him to sit down. He went and faced her. Sitting down and staring while admiring her exquisite interior design work. Vance gave a nod. Impressed by her choice of style. She waved it off like a small gesture of good fortune.

"You may be wondering why I took you from those hybrids and why you're here."

"I am wondering? What was the reason. How come you're different than your crew?"

"Because they've learned to respect me."

"I guess you were just a woman looking to do something others refused?"

"Refused is a slight word to use in my line of work. No, they did not refuse, yet, they didn't survive the pathways."

"Survive?"

"Most of the people on this planet strive to live. It is a necessary evil one must do in order to obtain food, water, and supplies to maintain their lives. The majority on this planet have even scraps to survive. To make amends to their gods and to keep their families safe. The some, they only seek to acquire whatever it is they need and they're content. So they shall be. But, the few. Oh, the few. The few do what they must to survive. Even if they have to slaughter, make war, or enter conflict with the others. In the end, the few have always won. Vanok is their world and not the other way around."

Vance nodded slowly, taking in her words.

"And you happened to be one of the few?"

"I am now. Before I was one of the majority. My mother and father did what they could to give me a proper childhood. However, war had fallen and my father went into battle. He survived the conflict, of course. But, his health declined due to the weapons used in the war. Chemicals that have transferred the sky above into the warping it appears today. Afterwards, my mother took care of me until I was able to take care of myself. I learned as I traveled the two continents. Searching for new ways of work and opportunity. The majority had always preached to me that marriage was in my future. That I would find a man who I would be suitable to match. Funny, after all the men I've encountered, none of them saw me as wife potential."

"I'm sorry to hear that." Vance said slowly.

"Don't be. It taught me something important. As I learned the true nature of this world, I became one of the Some. Learning new things and new ways to make things work. I tried to tell those I knew in my past abut these things and they refused. Saying, 'You can't live like that. It's too difficult to make such a path. The carving would be detrimental to one's own health.'. Crazy stuff they believe. Yet, that's what holds them down. Holds them back from increasing themselves. Elevating one's self is a sure way to make a move in this world."

"And what kind of carving did you make for yourself in this world?"

"First off, was military duty. I served in the Navy of the Kingdom of Vetoria. Fought countless battles on and off the seas. Most of my conflict was with the hybrids. We are taught in the forces the hybrids are responsible for more of the planet's dire circumstances. The increasing of the seas and the warping sky. All caused by their existence. The Navy's task was to eliminate any hybrids we encountered. And so we did."

"So, now you lead a group of pirates to do what exactly? Hold on. Is that why you ambushed the ship and took me?"

"Yes and no. Yes as in I ambushed the ship because they were hybrids. It's in my nature now. And no. I did not attack them simply to take you. Well, I didn't know you were onboard to start with. My intentions were simply elsewhere. That is until I saw you myself. From that point I had to take you."

"But why?"

"You're not a Vanokian. That much is true. Your essence oozes off your body. Your spirit's scent emits from you like a foreign soul."

"You know I'm not from this planet then."

"Certainly. What I want to know is why did you come here? What attracted you to Vanok in the first place?"

"First off, I didn't even know there was a Vanok to begin with. I was simply traveling through a wormhole and I ended up here. That is what happened."

"Truly?"

"Yes. Otherwise I would've had directions to go. I had no directions other than a wormhole."

"You said you're from Earth." The woman said, leaning in her chair. "Tell me, what is this Earth you speak of?"

"As I told the Captain of the Hybrids, Earth is the third planet from the sun. Second to Venus and first to Mars."

"I've never heard of Earth or Venus or Mars. They sound interesting though. That I'll give to you."

"I must be in a whole different solar system."

The woman reached down and picked up a map, she laid it out on the desk and slid it closer to Vance. He leaned over and looked. It was a map of a solar system. Yet not the one he is knowledgeable of. The planets on the map were bigger and the stars were brighter. Even it's sun was more of a darker fireball than the sun he knew.

"From what you're telling me, you most certainly are. Listen, this is what this system offers you. The first planet from the sun is what we like to call Firoh, a fiery planet. Its air will consume anything it touches. Second is Vanok, where we sit this day. A planet covered in much water and less land. Third is Jarok. A mysterious planet. We often wonder if there is life on it at all. Besides that, the tech capable of interstellar flight is kept in the secret chambers of the King of Vetoria. Fourth is what we call Arton, a planet covered in red dust. We speculate no life has been on that planet for millenniums. Fifth is Zutah, the planet of the Eye. Not sure what that means. Scholars here are still speculating. Sixth is Tharnog, surrounded with debris it gives off a bright light the father you're from it. You can slightly see it during the nights. Seven is Ocenia. Called that because it is known to be a planet of only water. No land."

"But, how are you certain of this? Of all of this?"

"Because of the scholars. They keep the records of the history of the system. The books have been around for ages."

Vance nodded, wiping the sweat from his forehead.

"This is a lot to take in."

"It has that affect on newcomers. But, don't you fret, there's still a lot more to learn."

"I see."

"Now, back to what I was saying. Oh, yeah. Now. The eighth planet is called Poston, somewhat similar to Oceania in appearance. However, instead of roaring waters, suffocating mists."

"I'm not certain as to how that works."

"You breath it in, you die. Simple as that."

Vance looked at the map again, seeing two remaining planets. The one after Poston was smaller and white as snow. The planet after was as dark as coal. the two planets seemed to mirror each other, according to Vance's understanding. The woman noticed his interest in the two planets as she smiled and tossing back her long wavy hair.

"Those two are enigmas of their own."

"And why is that?"

"The one before is called Hailon, a planet covered in dense snow. Often times, the scholars believe its pouring snow every second of a day. Can you imagine, nonstop snowfall for the rest of your days?"

"No I cannot. Where I live, snow is a rare occasion. Often appearances. But, rare."

"You're saying it doesn't snow on Earth?"

"No. It snows. Yes. But, not everywhere gets it. Only portions receive it. If you understand what I'm trying to say."

"I hear you."

"Does it snow here? In these waters?"

"Several times during the Sapphire Cycle. But, that's a whole 'nother tale."

"And what of the last planet? It looks a bit eerie."

"Because it is. We call that one simply Abyssian."

"Abyssian?" Vance said. "Like the abyss?"

"Why else name it after."

The woman sighed as she glanced over to a clock which sat against the ship walls. Seeing the time, she stood up and called for her pirates to return. Entering the study, they surround Vance and hold him up as he begins asking more questions concerning his fate. The woman laughed as she approached him closely.

"At least tell me what you want from me?"

"Oh. I want nothing from you. But, I know someone who will."

"I'm not understanding."

"We're on our way to the Kingdom of Vetoria. The King will like to have a word with you."

"The King?" Vance asked. "Why me?"

"Because you're the first being to come from another planet in ages. Such an event is one the King would not like to miss."

"Hold on. How does he know I'm here?"

"We have our ways of contact. Remember me saying something about tech earlier. It works in many ways. Ways the Majority will never come to understand and the Some refuse to use in order to advance themselves."

The woman commanded the pirates to take Vance to the guest room on the ship. Dragging him down the hallway, they opened the door and tossed Vance inside. Shutting the door before he could make a turn-around. Vance looked at the room, seeing a bed, a dining table, and a shelf of books. He looked over toward the shelf, looking at the books' spines, reading the titles. They were a mystery to him. All spoke about constellations and mysticism. Something Vance is not of interest in. While he were searching through, a knock came from the door, startling him. He stood up from his knees and called out tot eh visitor. The door had opened and it was the woman. Closing the door behind her as Vance stood confused.

"Why are you putting me in here?"

"To give you some comfort before you meet the King."

"None of this is making sense."

"I can't treat you like a slave and bring you to the King. He'll see the way you were treated and make a conclusion from that point. He has ways which are peculiar to foreigners."

Vance nodded while sitting down at the dining table. The woman looked and nodded. Something came to her attention. She called her hands, startling Vance as she laughed. He shook his head, trying to keep his composure and mental state. This is a day he never expected to live. But, here he is.

"Very well. I'll have some food brought to you and you can take a moment to rest before you meet the King."

"Well, thank you for your sudden hospitality. Could've doe this earlier and I may have taken you differently."

"The day is not over and I am not easy to comprehend. Nor are my motives."

The woman turned to exit the room, but Vance called out to her. Catching himself before even thinking of what to say next. She stood still, waiting for Vance to speak. He nodded and had a thought. A simple one.

"You never told me your name? That is if you have one."

"My name." she said. "You want to know my name?"

"I would like to. Otherwise, I would have to refer to you as the woman who took me from the ship or the Invader."

"As much as I would prefer those two, I'll tell you my name. although, I must warn you. Not even my crew knows of my name and for your sake, I would like to keep it that way."

"Wait, how do they not your name? so, they simply call you Captain?"

"Captain is enough for them to know who I am and my worth."

Vance nodded in agreement. He understood her intentions for once. The woman took a breath before uttering another word. Something which took Vance off his guard. Seeing a slightly vulnerable state from the woman who invaded another's ship and fought off the hybrids before taking him.

"Calypso is my name."

"Calypso." Vance said. "Sounds, a little frightening."

"As it should be."

Calypso turned and left the room, leaving Vance in a frozen state of worry and insight. Vance sighed as he could hear the waves moving across the seas.

CHAPTER 4: THE KINGDOM OF VETORIA

Vance woke up to the waves and the running sounds of the pirates heading toward the deck. Getting himself up, he rushed outside the room and followed the pirates, leading him to the deck where Calypso stood. She looked out to her crew and saw Vance in the distance. She smirked with a nod. Turning around, she faced the direction and toward them was the Kingdom of Vetoria. She held up her hands, shouting a war cry in Vanokian dialect to which all the pirates rallied with her while Vance stood confused. Calypso approached Vance as he began ask her of the war cry.

"I said, Hail Vetoria. Hail to the gods."

"Oh." Vance replied. "I thought it was something of the likes of taking over the city."

"I couldn't do that to the King. However, I could if I chose to."

The ship made its way toward the landing deck as the pirates tossed over the anchor. Jumping off the ship, Calypso kept Vance close to her in avoiding the Vetorians who saw them arrive, staring at them like guard dogs protecting their home. Vance stared at them, even to the degree of Calypso warning him not to cause a scene. The Vetorian people were dressed modestly. The men wore slacks and long-sleeve robes in which reminded Vance of the Ancient Greek imagery. The women were fully dressed from head to toe decked in dresses and head coverings. Even to Vance's surprise, he happened to notice the women did not wear any makeup. He rubbed his eyes looking closer as he passed them by. Calypso noticed his interest and tugged him.

"What are you doing?"

"They're not wearing makeup."

"Makeup?" Calypso said. "What is makeup?"

"The women I knew, they would design their faces. Making them look more appealing."

Calypso scoffed.

"Is that what they do on Jarok? They paint their faces like the jesters of the court?"

"When you put it that way, maybe." Vance shrugged.

The overall landscape of Vetoria was one of a beautifully appearance. Attractive to the yes were its polished grounds and structures. Merchants passed them by on marble-like wagons and carriages. Even the animals passing by were of a different breed. Vance thought them to be cows, but given a much closer examination he spotted black dots across the back of the animals. From the carved designs of their gods scattered around and nearby the palace to the monuments inscribed concerning Vetorian laws and guidelines.

They approached the entry point to the Vetorian Palace. The monumental structure detailed in much sapphire and built with a light blue stone. The paint covered across the palace was nearly transparent to the waters which roared nearby. Vance also realized the air was different than the island of Aphro, much smoother and the sky was much clearer. Clear to the point, Vance could see the stars peeking through the thin clouds. The palace doors opened with two guards standing by. Wielding tridents in their right hands. The guards nodded toward Calypso and her two close pirate guards as they gave Vance a stare. A look of uncertainty as Vance nodded to them. They did not respond. Entering the throne room, Calypso looked ahead, seeing the King sitting. She stopped herself and turned to Vance as he noticed the King. The King himself wore the diverse garb of land and sea. From the hides of the beasts of the land to the teeth and scales from the creatures of the seas. However, his crown was made of pure sapphire and his staff was made of pure emerald.

Yet, there was gold layered upon his throne. Vance saw it and only shook his head. He has never seen so much sapphire, emerald, or even gold in his life. It was all just a dream to him.

"Before we enter, do what I say."

"Like what? Bow before him and don't give eye contact?"

"Exactly. You're smarter than you look, Jarokian."

Walking into the throne room, a room decorated with sapphire floors and ceilings. Painting layered across the walls detail a history of the planet. Vance stared at them. Seeing everything from pirates at war with royal navies, marriages, and even monsters from the seas clashing with enlightened beings coming down from the sky. The King saw them and smiled. waving toward Calypso as he stood up and hugged her. He greeted the two pirate guards and paused, looking at Vance. His eyes slanted over toward calypso with question. She nodded with a smile.

"I can explain this man's unknown arrival."

"Do explain."

The King sat down as Calypso began to explain Vance's reasoning for standing in his throne room. Calypso introduced Vance to the King, King Kharan. Vance waved to no reply from Kharan. Calypso told the king of Vance's possible value to his kingdom and what he can do in order to achieve a place in the Vetorian landscape. Calypso even pointed out the details of Vance's arrival from another planet. Kharan asked what planet did Vance originate from and Vance held his hand up to their surprise.

"Earth. I come from Earth."

"What is Earth?" Kharan asked Calypso. "I've never heard of this Earth before?"

"He speaks of Jarok, my King." Calypso answered. "This man is a native to Jarok. He came here by ship."

"Jarok. You came from the planet after us?"

"I did, King Kharan. Where I'm from, we call it Earth. It's simple."

"So it may be. Tell me, why come here? Why not traverse the stars and reach a planet filled with a much greater life than exists here? A planet with much land and sea for everyone to share?"

"To be honest, I wasn't even sure where I was headed. I traveled and discovered a wormhole and from there I arrived here. Or crashed here. However you perceive the arrival."

"And what do you intend to do from this point forward?"

"I would like to return home eventually. To tell everyone I know about this place."

"And tell them why? To entice some to war. If you could travel here through a one-way tunnel, then so could they. War is not what we need in this day and hour. We already have enough conflicts with the hybrids that roam the lands and scavenge the seas. From what I can sense, you had a confrontation with them."

"Not as much as a confrontation. More like a meeting without knowing."

"Calypso, my dear. Where did you find this man?"

"I found him on the ship of the Captain of the Hybrids."

"He was with them?" Kharan said, standing up from his seat. "And you brought him here?"

"It's not like that, my King."

"Then how is it?"

"I attacked their ship as you commanded all of us to do. While ambushing, I discovered Vance on the ship. To me, he appeared to be a slave to the Captain. He wasn't around the others nor did he act like them. His countenance told me he was of potential and that is why he's standing here before you."

Kharan sat back down and scratched his beard. Giving both Vance and Calypso eyes of questioning. Calypso hung her head while Vance looked around at the throne room's design. Taking another look at the paintings and smiled.

"Who designed those?"

"An artist who spent much time in Vetoria. He still does paintings for us this day."

"That's cool. Can I meet him?"

"No."

"Fair enough."

Kharan sighed, looking toward Calypso and Vance.

"I have a proposition for you. The both of you actually."

"I'm all ears." Vance said.

"What is it, my King?"

"I will see what this Jarokian can do. I will test his might, his skill, his mentality, and lastly, his spirit. I want to see if the people of Jarok are as, stable as the legends tell them to be."

"Wait. You said legends."

"I did."

"You mean you're aware on life on Earth. I mean Jarok?"

"I do. Many of the scrolls kept in the achieves chamber by my scholar have indicated the people of Jarok are somewhat above us. In skill, technology, and spirituality."

"I wouldn't put us up to that kind of stature. But, I see your concerns."

"But, since you're from Jarok. Are the people as the legends say or are they less?"

"It's complicated to say the least. Some are and some aren't."

"Depends on where one goes, doesn't it?" Kharan asked.

"It does."

"Hmm. Well then, time will reveal all things. This man seems to have some potential indeed, Calypso."

"He will not prove you wrong, my King. I am positive he has the skills capable of cleansing this planet of the hybrids just as you desire."

"We shall see once the tests are complete. Maybe your words prove right about this man, Calypso. However, maybe you're wrong. But in the end, it is this man who will provide us all with the answer."

While they spoke, the sound of a door opening creaked behind Kharan. He stood up and looked back, seeing a young woman entering the throne room. Kharan smiled as Calypso bowed and Vance stood still. Staring at the young woman. Dressed in red apparel from her neck down. She wore golden rings on her fingers and layered gold laced within her dress. She even had a golden tiara and necklace to match.

"Vance Harlan of Jarok, allow me to introduce to you my daughter, Serilda. She has been praying for a warrior to arrive to aid her father in his conquest of ridding this planet of the hybrids. Perhaps, you are that warrior. Perhaps, my daughter's prayers have been answered by the gods."

Vance nodded to Serilda and she nodded back. Yet, their eyes had locked with one another and immediately Vance was pulled into a void. A void unseen by anyone else in the throne room. Vance moved throughout the void, leaning he was outside of his body as he turned around seeing himself, Calypso, Serilda, and Kharan standing in the throne room.

"What is going on?"

"I have prayed for you to come." A voice said within the void.

"Prayed for me? I'm not understanding what you ask of me."

"You can be the light to Vanok. The pathway to a new world. A world where Vetorians and hybrids can live as one. As one people."

"Listen, I'm just a man. I don't fight wars for conquest that are beyond my comprehension. This isn't even my home."

"But, you are here for a reason. A reason which has been chosen well by the gods."

"I don't know these gods."

"In time, you will come to know. Everyone on Vanok does eventually. Now wake up."

Within seconds, Vance awoke to find himself standing in the same place and his eyes were still locked on Serilda. However, when Vance came to the understanding of the sudden void, Serilda gave him a smirk before she took her leave. Kharan stepped forward toward Vance, placing his hand on his shoulders. Kharan turned to Calypso.

"Calypso, I will take him from here. I'm sure there are a plenty things you have to attend to."

"Yes, my king. I do have one question. If I may ask."

"Speak."

"The Captain of the Hybrids will soon be coming for Vance

Harlan. The sense in the air tells me he'll be making his way here to find him."

"And you want me to grant you permission to face him head-on?"

"If you would like him out of your hairs, then yes."

Kharan nodded with a grin.

"Good. Good. Go and cleanse our waters of the hybrid filth. Return to me when the task is complete. A reward will be waiting for you when you arrive."

"I will do as you command."

"Vance Harlan of Jarok. My guards will bring you to one of our luxurious rooms. You will stay here for the night as your tests will begin on the morrow. Best to rest yourself before the trails of your life begin."

Calypso bowed before she made her leave as the Vetorian guards escorted Vance to one of the guest rooms of the palace. Arriving at the room, Vance immediately noticed the layout of the room. Reminding him of the wealthy places to stay on Earth. From a nice balcony overlooking the city and the sea to the decorated furniture. Even the air was cleaner than the outside. The guards left Vance as he sat down gazing out toward the city, hearing the voices of the people mixed with the rushing waters of the sea.

Elsewhere on the seas, the Captain of the Hybrids sat down in his study, overlooking the map with a marking directed onto the Kingdom of Vetoria. From the study doors entered one of the hybrids. A being which looked to be a leopard mixed with a human. The leopard portion on the upper body and the human portion on the lower.

"Boss, we've received word from the others."

"What is this word?"

"They've said to have seen the foreigner. The one who fell from the sky."

"Have they? And where did they see him?"

"Vetorian sir. He was escorted by Calypso toward the palace."

The Captain raised his head from the map. Rolling up the map and setting it aside. He laid back in his chair as he thought to himself. He raised himself up back to the desk and opened the map again, this time staring at the red markings over Vetoria.

"So, she means to make him a tool of war for Kharan, huh. Well then, I guess they won't be expecting us when we arrive. They want war. Let's give them a war."

CHAPTER 5: A TEST OF FORTITUDE AND KNOWLEDGE

Vance arose to the sound of the waters as he gazed outside, seeing the Vetorian people going about their day as they did before. Taking in the scenery, a knock thundered from the door. Vance turned around, speaking for the visitor to enter. The door opened as Kharan himself entered the room. Vance saw him and nodded his head in reverence.

"I take it you received a well night's rest?"

"I did. One I haven't had in a long time."

"Very well. That is good to hear. Because you will require all the energy you can muster this day. For it will be a challenging one."

"What kind of trials are set for me today?"

"A variety of sorts. First, prepare yourself. Eat well and my guards will bring you to the arena for the first trial."

"Arena?" Vance paused. "Like a fighting arena?"

"Are there any others?"

"I see."

"You will once you arrive. Take this time, Vance Harlan of Jarok. Take it well."

Kharan exited the room, leaving Vance to take the moment to prepare himself. Vance had sighed, gazing back out to the open area of the city. From there, Vance knelt down near the bed and began to pray. He prayed for protection against any adversary which may be awaiting him at the arena. Afterwards, Vance ate the breakfast which was delivered to him immediately after his prayer. Once he was finished, a knock came from the door. Vance went and opened it, seeing two guards. He nodded and exited the room. Walking with them down the hall and followed them toward the arena. The arena itself was over thirty stories and there was no audience sitting in attendance, just yet. Standing in the middle of the arena was Kharan as he applauded Vance's arrival.

"You have come. Good. Good. Now, are you ready to hear what is being presented to you?"

"Ready as I'll ever be."

"Then let us begin!"

The arena doors shut and around Vance were several men dressed in light blue robes. Their faces shrouded by their hoods. In their hands were scrolls, worn and torn. The men opened the scrolls and laid them on the table which sat before Vance. Eight scrolls in total. Kharan commanded for Vance to approach the table and read the first one. Vance went and read it. Strangely to him, the scrolls were written in Vanokian, but he was able to read them as if they were English.

"What is this?"

"The first test of knowledge." Kharan answered. "To test your mind and your history."

Vance read the scroll in detail. Gaining the understanding he needed to comprehend this first test. Kharan kept his sights on Vance, seeing his mannerisms and facial changes.

"What does it say?" Kharan asked.

"It asks me to describe the difference between your world and mine."

"Then, describe it."

"What is there to describe. From what I've seen since my time on this planet, their behaviors and the appearances of the people are no different than the ones back on Earth. In a creepy way, they're both very similar."

Kharan nodded. He waved his hand toward the hooded one, who rolled up the first scroll and stood aside. Vance turned toward the second scroll and read it. Kharan asked Vance to speak what it says.

"This one asks of me to detail the differences between the skies between your world and mine."

"Tell us, what are those differences?"

"For starters, Earth's sky is not contaminated by the celestial storms I see above us."

"Then what is it contaminated by?"

"A variety of things. Matters to discuss in a greater detail which would take up my time on this test."

"I see." Kharan noted.

The second hooded one rolled up the scroll and stood aside as Vance approached the third scroll.

"This one speaks of the difference between the arts of war."

"Arts of war." Kharan said. "This will prove useful. Tell us, what are the differences?"

"The difference is there are no differences." Vance answered. "War is the same wherever you go. No matter the species which dwells upon the planet."

"By such words, you confirm that war is eternal?"

"War is eternal. The struggle keeps civilizations going until the end of all things."

"Noted."

The scroll was rolled up and Vance approached the fourth. The fourth one detailed the similarities between the animals on Earth compared to Vanok. Kharan asked Vance to give the answer and Vance only sighed.

"So far, I've never encountered any hybrids until I came here."

"Interesting." Kharan replied. "You mean to tell me you've never seen any hybrids back on your planet?"

"None. I'm not saying they don't exist there. But, I've never encountered one."

"Good to hear. At least your world doesn't have to deal with the suffrage of those savage creatures. Seeking to destroy all you hold dear. Pillaging wherever they go. Such filth."

The fifth scroll was read and Vance took in the words. The words enticed him slightly as they pertained to the government rulings between both worlds. Kharan asked Vance to answer once more and Vance only replied by stating the governments between the two planets are not hat different. Pertaining to which country one visits to the individual in charge. Kharan nodded with intrigue. The sixth scroll was next to be read and upon the sixth scroll were two drawings. One of a man. Another of a woman. Kharan asked for Vance to give an answer to the question of the drawings. Vance looked at the drawings carefully.

"Without them both, the planet would be without those of dominion. It is the nature of the balance."

"Nature of the balance." Kharan said. "Interesting choice of wordplay. Next."

The seventh scroll was approached by Vance and detailed the societal order of both worlds. Vance quickly answered by saying the roles of man, woman, and child must remain in constant flow unless they deem the civilization itself to collapse and eventually end all that remains. Kharan took this words carefully, as it reminded him of how he became king. Through a much similar circumstance. The last scroll was approached and Vance stood still, taking in the question. Kharan stood boldly against the wall as Vance read the scroll.

"What does it say?" Kharan asked.

"It asks the question of honor between the two worlds. Honor is a must in all worlds. Without it, one will never see the days ahead. Only a quick and painful death awaits those who dishonor for a sport cause."

"Good words. Good words."

Kharan waved for the scrolls and the table to be removed from the arena floor. The scholars disappeared into the shadows circling them. Vance stood still as he began to hear the sound of doors opening and he gazed up to the seats, beginning to see the civilians enter the arena. Vance turned to Kharan, asking him what was about to happen. Kharan chuckled.

"Your next test. Combat."

"Combat?" Vance said. "Like right now?"

"Good place as any. Besides, you seem like a capable warrior who would defend himself if the cause came about. Now, the cause has arrived."

The guards entered the arena, tossing a rapier to Vance. He caught it and stared at the blade. Kharan walked toward him and handed him a firearm. Vance looked at the firearm and noticed there was something different.

"What kind of gun is this?"

"One you can only find within the walls of this palace. It will be of good use in your fights."

"But, how does it work?"

"You mean to tell me your kind don't have such weapons back on Jarok?"

"Oh no. we do. We have a lot of them. All different shapes and sizes. But, I'm just curious as to how this one works."

'You see the trigger?"

"Yes."

"Then you know how it works."

The crowds gathered within the arena and cheered as Vance looked up toward them. The doors in front of Vance on the other end of the arena had opened and out of them walked out three men. Two were guards of the palace while the third one appeared to be a pirate. One of Calypso's Vance had thought to himself. Kharan commanded the battle to begin and the three opponents rushed toward Vance. Hesitant to make an attack, Vance deflected the swords of the guards and the pirate. The guards moved with such speed that Vance had to double his efforts to keep up with their attacks. The pirate stood back and scoffed at Vance's defensive skills while making an attack in between the guards' own. Vance swiped the blade, knocking one of the javelins out of the guard's hand before shoving him to the ground to the audience's excitement. Te second Guard went to make a strike, Vance dodged the attack and used the gun to blast a hole through the guard's chest. Vance caught himself as he looked at the firearm, recognizing it was an energy gun as it fired a bright blue beam through the guard's chest as if it was nothing. The pirate stood still, looking down at the guard's body and made a run for it. Vance sighed as he waved to the audience and their cheers calmed him. Kharan nodded and approached Vance from his seat.

"Excellent work. You have done well."

"I hope this is over with. I'm not sure I can kill another. That was an accident."

"An accident or a gesture of self-defense? If you had not fired the shot, they would've killed you."

Vance knew this and took it well. Kharan nodded and waved toward the door. The doors had opened and this time only one figure emerged from the shadows. Vance saw the figure, seeing it was a warrior clothed in greenish armor made from the scales of the sea creatures and in his hands he held a trident made of horns.

"You do however have one more battle." Kharan said. "Defeat him and you will enter the third and final portion of this test."

The audience roared as the gladiator entered the arena. Vance stood firm as his right hand was gripped onto the hilt of the rapier and his left hand was steady with the energy gun. The gladiator screamed to the audience's cheer as he ran toward Vance with the trident head-on. Vance moved out of the trident's path, slashing the blade across the gladiator's back. The blade impacted the armor, shattering small fragments of the scales. The gladiator paused and stared.

"It's a fight." Vance said. "What else am I supposed to do?"

The gladiator screamed, slamming the trident to the ground in front of Vance. He stepped back as the gladiator went for a punch, hitting Vance across his jaw as he pushed him to the ground. Vance looked around and fired a shot from the energy gun to the gladiator's chest. The armor shattered, but the beam did not pass through. Vance was surprised.

"You thought a beam could take me out?!" The gladiator yelled. "Do you know who I am?!"

"I'm afraid I don't." Vance replied. "Who are you supposed to be?"

"You fool! I am Batrion the Destroyer! This day, you will learn why I've earned it."

"I'm not so sure I will."

Batrion went for another strike with the trident and Vance fired a shot at Batrion's hand. Dropping the trident from the blast, he looked at his hand. Seeing the shredded scales and feeling the burning over his skin. Vance grinned.

"I'm learning."

Batrion went for a punch and Vance dodged the attack, instead swiping the blade atop Batrion's hand, cutting it off. Batrion yelled as he fell to his knees, holding his severed wrist as hi hand laid on the floor to the audience's surprise. Vance sighed.

"Please yield."

Batrion glared into Vance's eyes, going for another attack with Vance only hitting him in the head with the energy gun. Batrion collapsed to the ground as the audience cheered Vance's victory. Kharan applauded as he stood up and granted Vance the winner of the day's battle. The audience began to leave as Kharan stood still with the hooded figures making their return into the arena. Batrion himself was carried out by the guards and his hand was taken as well. The hooded figures surrounded both Kharan and Vance as Kharan began to lay out the final portion of the test. The third and final portion pertaining to spirituality.

"Spirituality?" Vance asked. "Like what about it?"

"We want to know. I want to know. What do you believe in? Are there any gods back on your world the people worship? How many do they worship?"

"Well, it all depends on where one travels."

"I see. So, in your area of living, how many gods to they serve?"

"Depends on who you ask. It's a mixed-multitude in the country I live in."

"So, you mean to tell me, there can be one who worships one god while the other can worship a plethora of gods and they live on the same field?"

"Yes. That's what it's like. Unless you buy out the land for yourself and those of your like-mindedness."

Kharan nodded.

"Interesting. Now, I must ask you this question and this one will ensure your future upon this planet and within my kingdom."

"I'm listening."

"How many gods do you serve?"

"Honestly. I serve one."

"One. You serve one god?"

"Yes I do."

"And those you've met on your travels back on your world? Others you've shared conversations with? How many gods have they claimed to serve?"

"Some several. Many a lot. Few only serve one god."

"Such an enigma back on your world. Do you not know that where there's more gods, the better?"

"I'm not sure that confirms the clarification of worship."

"And why do you say that?"

"Because, where I'm from and how I was raised. There was only one god. He created everything and everyone."

"Everything and everyone on your world?"

"No, your Majesty. He created all things. Even this world we stand on today. He created even you."

The scholars lifted up their heads, staring at Vance with hatred searing in their eyes. Vance caught them by the feeling of an unsettling energy moving around the arena. Kharan stood still, calmly taking in Vance's words.

"He is a destroyer." One scholar spoke.

"He will destroy all you have built!" A second scholar spoke.

"Dispose of him, my King." The third scholar spoke.

"He is a blasphemer to the gods!" The fourth scholar spoke.

"Death and fire will rain down over all of Vanok if he remains!" The fifth scholar spoke.

The following three scholar spoke their own minds as the first five continued to repeat their statements. Kharan shook his head and grabbed his staff, slamming it into the floor, causing a crack to form as the sound of a shockwave echoed through the arena field.

"Silence yourselves!" Kharan yelled. "I will deal with him in matters of my own making."

The scholars hung their heads and stepped back three steps. Kharan approached Vance, looking him in the eyes. He nodded.

"Very well. I see you stand by your belief. That is something I highly respect in any individual. For one who stands for their beliefs is one I would align myself with for any cause."

Vance nodded in respect to Kharan's honor. Kharan allowed Vance to return to his room as the test were complete. Vance had passed. The guards entered and brought Vance back to his room while the scholars continued to speak against him. Kharan heeded their words and commanded for them to remain silent. One scholar refused and proclaimed that the gods of Vanok would strike down Kharan if he not rid the kingdom of Vance. Kharan took his staff and smashed it across the scholar's head and beat him to death in front of the others. The remaining seven stood silent as Kharan commanded for his guards to take the scholar's body and toss it into the seas.

"What happens to Vance will be of my choice. My decision. Not the gods." Kharan proclaimed as he left the arena.

CHAPTER 6: PIRATES OF VANOK

The Captain of the Hybrids and his crew rode across the roaring seas, following the trail on the map. The Captain kept his gaze on the surroundings. Seeing nothing but water in his sights. Up ahead, one of the hybrids ran forward with binoculars, handing them to the Captain.

"Ahead, sir!"

The Captain looked on and saw Calypso's ship up ahead. He knew she was coming for him and he grinned. Looking further behind her, he could see land. He screamed toward his crew they have arrived on the continent of Vetor. The crew cheered as they prepared themselves for battle. Over on the other ship, Calypso looked out toward them with her crew ready as their swords were drawn.

"He continues to act as if he will survive the journey." Calypso said. "Well, he will realize his end is nigh by the sharpness of my blade."

The two ships reached one another as the battle began with the hybrids clashing with the pirates. This time, the hybrids allowed thee animalistic urges to consume them, in so much as slaughtering Calypso's pirates with a certain ease. Calypso herself was not bothered by their animal rages as she sliced her way through them to get to the Captain. She walked on the deck, killing hybrids as she saw the Captain waiting for her with his sword drawn and a smile on his face.

"You think this is funny?!"

"I do. I have a dark sense of humor."

Calypso and the Captain's blades clashed with the sound of

thunder above them. They locked eyes as the ongoing battles continued around them.

"Where did you take the foreigner?"

"None of your concern."

"It is of my concern. I was the one who found him first!"

"You would've wasted his potential! His skill!"

"I would've?! You took him to your king, didn't you?!"

The Captain swiped the sword as Calypso deflected the blade with her own. The two circled one another while taking out one from the other's crew. Their eyes still locked onto each other as rain began to pour down upon them. The Captain laughed, taking in the scenery.

"The Jarokian will prove a useful ally to the King in ridding this planet of your crew's kind. Such nature cannot allow to continue."

"Who gave you the right to determine who lives and who dies?! Your King?!"

Calypso nodded.

"It's my job."

"Kill me and my crew here and now, and maybe we'll see if it's your job."

Calypso screamed as she rushed against the Captain with her sword. The two battled on the deck in the midst of their crews. The Captain laughed continually as Calypso screamed like a siren. The blades clashed and clashed as sparks flew from them. Calypso twirled the blade and kicked the Captain in the abdomen as he fell. Rushing over to impale him, one of the hybrids jumped onto Calypso's back, biting her in the shoulder. She screamed as she plunged the blade into the hybrid's chest. The Captain arose and fought back against Calypso. More hybrids went to intervene, only to be killed by Calypso's blade. The captain kept fighting as several of Calypso's pirates moved in to attack him. Only for his hybrids ambush them by biting their necks or impaling them with their tails.

"You cannot win." Calypso said. "You have no right."

"Again, who gave you the right to determine who wins and who loses? Oh, that's right. Your job."

Calypso went to strike the Captain again, yet, a large lightning bolt crashed into the waters. Startling everyone, even the Captain as he made his move toward the wheel of the ship. Calypso looked around, seeing everyone returning to their own ships. Even her crew was afraid.

"Where are you going?!" This battle is not over!"

"We must go, my lady!" One of her pirates said. "The gods, they're angry at us all. We're in danger if we stay out here!"

"You'll be in danger if you allow those savages to live!"

She stood over the edge of the hybrid's ship against her own. Calypso turned around as the Captain dropkicked her back onto her ship as his ship made their escape. Standing up in haste, she looked out seeing the hybrids' ship heading towards Vetor. Screaming in anger, she turned her attention toward her crew. Yelling for them to fight back against the hybrids. However, some refused stating the lightning bolt was a sign of a truce between the two forces. Believing the gods have called off the ongoing war. Calypso scoffed as she dug her blade into several of their chests. She looked at the remaining members of her crew.

"If you are not with me, then you are not with your King!"

The crew stared at her with fear. Uncertain for their lives as they saw her take out several of their own crew members. She walked in front of them, wielding the blood-soaked sword in their faces. The blood brought forth another essence of fear upon them. For they were more afraid of Calypso now than before.

"Make your choice now. Are you with me? Are you with the King? Or are you with those savages?"

The crew yelled they were with her and the king. Calypso nodded as she commanded them to toss the dead bodies over into the seas. Obeying her word, once the bodies fell into the waters, a massive sea creature arose, covered in dark emerald-like scales and its eyes were as bright as the sun. The beast gazed around the waters, seeing the bodies and took them deep into the seas with its mouth. The crew saw it and fell for fear as Calypso grinned, seeing it as a sign of their coming victory.

CHAPTER 7: A WAY HOME?

Vance walked through the palace after being given permission by Kharan. He was astounded by the architecture. By walking through the corridors, he was able to see more of the interior. Along his walk, he discovered more paintings across the walls. Only these walls depicted a great war between the hybrids and the royals. One of the figures in the painting was Kharan himself wielding a glowing trident made of sapphire. The trident was struck by lightning as he was clashing against a hybrid beast of man, lion, and serpent. Continuing his walk, Vance ran into Serilda, startling her and himself.

"Wasn't expecting to see you here." Vance said. "Especially during this time of night."

"I am the Princess. Therefore, I have permission to gad abroad."

"So I can see."

"It appears you have completed my father's tests."

"I did. And not to my liking. Although, his tests were a bit strange for me. Not that I am a fighter by any means. The knowledge tests with the scrolls was easy for me to overcome. The combat however, that was a challenge."

"And the spiritual test? Was that as challenging as well?"

"It was easy. Tough but easy."

"Explain to me how it was tough? And why?"

"Because, I don't speak much on my beliefs. Personality, I would prefer to keep them t myself. To avoid conflict."

"That's funny."

"How so?"

"Because we're taught to speak highly of our beliefs. It is those in which make us who we are. The things we do and the words we speak rely solely on the beliefs we share. If it were not for them, we would be vagabonds in the end. Heretics to a fallen cause."

Vance held his composure. He was amazed by the speech of a princess. Much less one who appeared physically to be so intelligent. Vance applauded her words of wisdom.

"You speak well. For someone like yourself."

"And they don't have women like me back on your world?"

"Women like you are a dying breed where I'm from. Although, there are a few every now and then. Scattered like the sands of the sea."

"Touching."

"It can't be all that bad." Vance said. "Seeing as how you're who you are. Your father must've done something well."

"He takes care of me and his people. It is his duty as king and as a father."

"Where is your mother?"

"She went off on some diplomatic duties to the west. The Kingdom of Nabel needed her guidance toward their concern regarding their women. My mother is skilled in setting places straight. To keep the balance in play."

"That's something worth knowing."

"I could tell you sense my father's rulings a bit harsh."

"In a sense. The ways he views the hybrids is something unnecessary. The hybrids only want to live in peace. They do not seek to fight."

"And how do you know this? Last I heard, you were aboard their ship. Possibly taken captive."

"No. I wasn't taken captive. They saved me."

"Saved you? From what?"

"My ship crashed. I was stranded on an island, and they arrived. Brought me in and treated me well. As best they could before they were attacked by Calypso and her crew."

"Ah, Calypso." Serilda said. "I'm surprised she still is seen in good spirits toward my father."

"Calypso told me she does well for your father's kingdom. She despises the hybrids just as much as he does."

"That much is certain. However, Calypso sees much more in this field of war than slaughtering any hybrids she comes across. She wants a place to rule."

"How are you aware of this?"

"Because I've been in council meetings before. Where she would be welcomed. Her words always spoke of some kind of rule. Whether it was an island to call her own or a kingdom to dwell. Ruler-ship is something is craves deeply and the killing of hybrids will not cease that desire."

"I see why she's the way she is."

"Anyhow, why are you walking through the halls of the palace?"

"Just taking a gander of things. I saw the painting in the throne room when I first arrived. Didn't know there were many more scattered throughout the place."

"You should check the library. There's much in there to grab your attention."

"There's a library here?"

"Of course. I will take you to it."

From there, Vance followed Serilda through several sets of corridors, passing by the guards who stood like statues. Entering the western portion of the palace, Serilda opened the large double-doors which appeared to be made of wood layered with coral. Within the room was the library. Nearly three floors filled with scrolls and maps. Scattered in the library were small statuettes of ships pertaining to Kharan's Navy and the Navy before his rule. Vance stood at the entrance, shaking his head in wonder.

"Endless amounts of scrolls."

"Indeed." Serilda chuckled. "Besides, only those permitted to the palace can step foot in this place."

"You mean the people outside have no entry into this library? For what cause?"

"It's a royal decree. The people have the Library of Vetoria to themselves within the city."

"But, what's the difference between them? One gets standard information while the other gains a little extra note."

"Some matters of this continent's history must be protected by the royals. It is the decree of the ancients. Their rule and my father continues it to this day."

Vance walked through the library, seeing the shelves of scrolls. Each shelf was detailed with a description. Some were focused on architecture. Others weaponry, history, technology, societal science, oceanography, cosmology, artistry, and spirituality. Serilda watched as Vance gazed at the shelves.

"If you're behavior like this over some scrolls, I can only imagine your reaction to the Science Hall."

"Science Hall?"

"Follow me."

He followed Serilda down another set of corridors, taking them to the northwest portion of the palace where the Science Hall remained. The doors were opened as Vance saw the technology without haste. The walls were layered with the energy guns. All in the shapes of handguns, rifles, machine guns, and even Gatling guns. Also on the wall were hung swords, staves, javelins, axes, maces, and three tridents. Each one a different design than the other. Serilda began to describe to him the purpose of the hall and how the technologists each operate within the hall unaware of those in or out of the palace. While she showed Vance around, a guard stepped forward at the entrance, calling for Serilda.

"Yes?"

"Your father requires your presence at the throne room."

"I'm on my way."

The guard made his leave as Serilda told Vance to continue looking around. He wouldn't have to worry about a thing with Serilda speaking for him. Serilda had left and Vance walked through the hall. Seeing the weapons and further through the hall, he saw the structure which he knew would be used to layer out the ships for the Navy. Further down, he caught the glimpse of something larger. Entering the hall, spotting the ceiling inching higher than before.

Vance looked and saw his ship sitting in the larger room.

"How did they find this?"

Vance ran toward the ship and looked at it. The ship was polished. No cracks. No broken glass. The ship was restored. Vance stepped up the ladder and pressed the ignition and the ship activated. The ship was fully repaired. Vance took the moment to think. Now he can return to Earth. Vance looked ahead in the ship's targeted direction, seeing a pathway which led to the outside of the palace. The ship could take off and make the escape from there. Vance took the second to conjure a plan. While he planned his next move, the Captain of the Hybrids arrived in the city with his hybrids and they quickly made haste toward the palace. Clashing against the guards at every turn. Kharan is warned of their arrival as he spoke with Serilda. Kharan stood up from his throne and snatched his staff from the side of the seat.

"Remain in here until it is clear."

"Yes, Father."

Kharan's Navy battled the Captain and his hybrids during the nightfall as the people of the city slept. That is until they heard the bells gong and they awoke to the sound of battle cries and clashing swords. The people began to evacuate from the city and head into the country land, which was set outside of the city's jurisdiction. Some chose to evacuate by jumping into boats of their own. While they did, they were caught in a stumble as Calypso and her crew made their return. Jumping from their ship into the battle. Calypso moved with fierce as she searched the surroundings for the Captain. Unable to find him on the outside, she turned her focus toward the palace and made her steps there. Inside the science hall, Vance could hear the sounds of the battle taking place as he looked back and forth between his ship and the sounds of the swords.

CHAPTER 8: THE VANOKIAN PATH

The battles continued outside between the hybrids, Calypso's pirates, and Kharan's Navy Guards. Meanwhile, inside the palace. Kharan waited in the gardens as the Captain of the Hybrids arrived. Moving with speed as he stopped himself, seeing the King. The Captain stepped forward into the garden. Seeing the plants growing across the walls, as if they were hung there from the start. The Captain pointed and scoffed.

"Must be some work to get this done."

"Why are you here?"

"Why am I here? Because I'm looking. Looking for a friend of mine. The Jarokian."

"The Jarokian is here under my authority. What do you seek with him?"

"Um, what do I seek? Uh, a chance to speak with him. Tell him to choose his path."

"What path?"

"Simple. He can either come with me and help the hybrids reclaim their territory or he can remain with you and eventually die under your rule."

"The Jarokian can handle himself. I've seen it firsthand."

"So, he can fight!" The Captain yelled. "That's even better. I knew he had it in him!"

Kharan slammed his staff into the ground and quickly before the Captain's sights, the staff transformed into a trident. The trident sparked with lightning as thunder roared from above.

"Such legends are true I see."

"Leave my palace!" Kharan yelled. "Take your hybrids with you before I have them all killed."

"Good sir, they are well prepared to die. Just as I."

The Captain's rapier clashed against Kharan's trident as the lightning traveled across weapons, shocking the Captain's hand. Kharan grinned as he twirled the trident and struck it into the ground, causing the lightning to move with speed and strike at the Captain's feet. He jumped over the bolts before they turned back toward him. He grabbed his rapier and scrapped the ground, taking the lightning onto his blade and holding it out toward Kharan.

"I know a few tricks as well."

The two faced off as Calypso rushed into the garden, seeing them staring down with both weapons pointed. She screamed for the Captain as she ran toward him with sword in hand. The Captain moved out of her path as Kharan threw his trident toward the Captain. He looked back and ducked own as the trident struck into the marble wall. He laughed.

"Two against one?! That's not fair. You need help."

The three of them looked at each other. The trident bolted back as the Captain ducked quickly, seeing the trident return to Kharan's hand. The Captain never seen a weapon do such a thing and took his leave. Calypso ran after him. While she chased him, Vance entered the battle, clashing against the guards and aiding the hybrids. Calypso saw him and anger fueled her as she ran toward him.

"You help them?!"

"I have to. It must be done."

"You choose the path of the Majority! For what cause have you grown such a hatred for yourself?!"

"It's not hatred. It's honesty."

"Then you know I have to kill you."

"I know you'll try. But, this night will not e the time."

Calypso glared toward Vance as the sound of an explosion shook the city. Calypso turned back, seeing how the explosion erupted from the palace as she ran inside. The guards followed as the hybrids made their escape. Vance escorted them back to their ship as he saw the

Captain retreating from the palace. He rushed toward him.

"The Jarokian still lives!"

"What just happened?"

"I set off something that might get their attention. I see you are helping my crew."

"I am."

"Then you are with us?"

"I am."

"Then get onboard! Before the guards return."

Vance jumped onto the ship as they made their escape. The following morning, the city streets were filed with dead guards, pirates, and hybrids. Kharan called for a search for Vance, believing him to have been taken by the Captain. Although, Calypso's words urged him to find Vance and kill him since she believes he was the cause for the explosion. Serilda stood back and watched the conversation between her father and Calypso. While they spoke, the guards entered.

"My King. You have visitors."

"Visitors?" Kharan said with confusion. "Bring them in."

At the entrance to the throne room came three men. Dressed in fine robes of silver. Their eyes were as pale as the moon and their demeanor was one of a foreign stature. They bowed before Kharan, showing him reverence.

"Who are you?"

"We come from a place afar. We seek someone who is here unwillingly and uninvited."

"Who do you speak of?" Calypso asked.

"We know of the Jarokian. Of how he came on this planet and the actins he's done. We even know of his blasphemous believes toward the gods."

"Just why are you searching fro him?" Kharan wondered.

"Because he is a disruption to the balance. He must be found before the dark forces of Vanok arise and consume you all."

"How do the three of you know all of this?" Calypso questioned. "Where are you from?"

"Again, we're from a place afar. Find the Jarokian before the dark forces begin to return."

The three robed ones left the throne room, leaving Kharan and Calypso lost for words. Meanwhile, Vance stood out on the deck of the ship as they headed out into the open seas. The Captain walked over toward him, holding a map.

"Where are we headed?" Vance asked.

"A little place south of Aphro. There's some things there that must be done."

"I understand."

Vance looked out toward the sea and nodded. He knew he would be on Vanok for a while. A new life. A new adventure awaited.

PRAXUS OF LITHONIA

CHAPTER I

In the early years, there was a kingdom.

A kingdom known as Bandoria.

Bandoria was a kingdom of great wealth and power as was its ruler, King Bantos. Many who had lived in Bandoria were truly successful in their lives, both personally and financially. Even though the rich had lived in Bandoria, there was another kingdom on the outskirts. A kingdom much smaller than the glory of Bandoria's towers and high walls. A kingdom which held a great many people. This kingdom is Lithonia. Lithonia was the sister kingdom to Bandoria, but did not share the rich and powerful delicacies of Bandoria's stature. Majority of the poor had dwelled in the walls of Lithonia, only due to the fact of not being allowed through the walls and onto the grounds of Bandoria.

One day, King Bantos had stepped out and gazed over the balcony of his palace. Looking out toward all the kingdom in its glory. As far out as his eye could wander. Glaring ahead, Bantos caught the glimmering light outside of the kingdom walls. He knew the light had sparked from Lithonia and his anger was quenched.

"This is my kingdom and these lands will belong to me." Bantos said toward his Vizier who stood beside him.

"My lord, what are your plans in overtaking the Lithonians from their kingdom? What of their king? What of their warriors?"

"We have hundreds of warriors prepped for battle, do we not?"

"Yes, my lord. Yes we do."

"Then we need not worry. That dirt-filled place they call a kingdom will be ours soon enough."

During these early years of the war between Bandoria and Lithonia, there was a great falling of many warriors on both sides. In another place within the boundaries of Lithonia, there was a woman who was known as Arinia who had given birth to a son. Her husband, Krotax, a warrior in the clan of Lithonians proclaimed his son's name as Praxus. A Lithonian name and in the Lithonian tongue meant *"ruler and conqueror"*. through the wars, they lived a happy life, even in the times of hardship and trouble from the Bandorian forces. They watched their son grow older through the conflicts.

Praxus himself in his youth became helpful to those in need as he watched Bandorian warriors invade their homes and slaughter the innocent. In one altercation, Praxus took it upon himself and slew two Bandorian warriors with his bare hands, proving to those who witnessed and his mother and father he possessed near superhuman strength. Once he became an adult, he volunteered in the battle against Bantos' forces and witnessed the death of his mother and father by Bantos' own hand. That day was the defeat of Lithnoia and it had fully become under the control of Bandoria.

Ever since their deaths, Praxus went into hiding in the undergrounds of Lithonia. Places Bantos and his advisors had possessed no knowledge of their existence. Gathering other mighty men and women of valor who saw Praxus' strength in times past. They came together and sought to overthrow Bantos and take by Lithonia for the people and to free the bonds of Bandoria from any other lands they may have conquered. Praxus made a vow to avenge the deaths of his people and his mother and father by killing Bantos himself and conquering Bandoria for the taking.

It all begins this day.

CHAPTER II

Now, Praxus and his small army of warriors had made their journey eastward, toward the Kingdom of Brithrow. A providence of Bandoria.

"What are we looking for, Praxus?" a soldier asked.

"Anything that could lead us to King Bantos." Praxus said.

"Then, why are we heading towards the Kingdom of Brithrow? I'm not sure on what you have planned."

"When we enter the gates of Brithrow, you'll see what my plans comes into being."

Riding along through the valleys, they come to a stop and find themselves facing the gates of the Kingdom of Brithrow. Standing by the gates are the Brithrowian Knights, dressed in their iron-clad armor and helmets. Their stained swords held in their hands and pressed against their chests. Their eyes are solely focused on Praxus and those of the Lithionian army. One knight made his way toward Praxus. Walking calmly, yet nervous.

"Might I ask why you have decided to come?"

"I've come to speak with your king." Praxus answered. "He and I are on good terms with one another and I would be pleased to speak to him."

The knight nodded and waved his right hand, signaling the knights to open the gates of the kingdom. The knights slowly open the gates as Praxus and his army enter into the kingdom. The residents of the kingdom look and see Praxus and his army coming through the kingdom, their horses moving with pace as they approached the castle of Brithrow's king, King Brithon. From the castle doors, walked out Brithon. His gaze looked around as he could hear the sounds of the horses and immediately turned to see Praxus and his army coming toward him.

"My, my. We have visitors." Brithon said.

Praxus' horse stopped in front of the castle. He looked at Brithon, whose standing at the doorway. Praxus gets off his horse and walked up the stony steps to approach Brithon. Brithon made his way to greet Praxus and they greet one another. As if they are close friends.

"Praxus of Lithonia has come to visit me."

"It is for an urgent matter."

"Come inside. We can talk there."

Praxus and Brithon enter into the castle walls as the Brithrow servants take Praxus' horse and his army's horses to their staples to rest up. The army followed the servants to the inside of the castle where they would be fed. Inside the castle, Praxus and Brithon talked about the current situations across the lands. Brithon already knows of the reasons for Praxus' rise in appearances ad why he's come to his kingdom on a short notice.

"I know why you've come here."

"Then you are aware that this is no time for any games to be played."

"I know you want to see King Bantos and his reign come to an end."

"I want his head impaled onto the tip of my sword."

"I figured as much. Which is why I have an offer for you concerning these dire matters."

"What is the offer you proposed?"

"That you aid me in your assistance against Bantos and his army. Granted, you know this Battle of Kings cannot last much longer."

Praxus thought to himself, detailing the proposal and what it would allow him to do, to get into Bandor and kill Bantos himself to avenge his parents' deaths. He nodded, facing Brithon. Praxus extended his arm in agreement.

"I shall assist you in this battle."

"Wonderful! When they see the two of us on the battlefield facing them, only fear will grab them by their throats and feed them to us."

"I do have one condition regarding this agreement of ours."

"Tell me."

"When we find Bantos, leave him to me."

Brithon nodded with a smile on face. He enjoys seeing the savagery coming through Praxus' words. He knew that he would be the right man to tag along with when it comes to war. Brithon extended his arm and the two came to an agreement. The deal was finalized.

"Agreed."

Praxus and his army remained within the Kingdom of Brithrow for the remainder of the day and spend the night within the kingdom. During those hours, Praxus and Brithon spoke to each other concerning the art of war and the use of weapons in the warfare. Praxus' army feasted and even laid with women that night. Praxus, on the other hand continue to have conversations with Brithon and they later went their separate ways to rest for the mission ahead.

CHAPTER III

The sun had risen and from the castle doors walked out Praxus and his army. They were prepared for the battle ahead. Brithon had approached Praxus from behind and patted him on his back. The two armies were easily to be told apart. Praxus' army dressed in simple garb. Loincloths of leather and fur with armbands and leather-padded boots. Some carried swords as the others wielded bows and arrows. Brithon's army were like a pack of wolves moving in a single-file line. Horned helmets and glistening armor. Swords bulging from their sides and arrows sharp on their backs.

"I surely hope that we can finish Bandor's army off before we come into conflict with him."

"Trust me, we will get through his army. They won't stand a chance."

Praxus and his army get atop their horses and gallop with Brithon and his army following them as they exit his kingdom. While they rode off, Praxus knew that Bantos was in his sights and he wouldn't let anyone or anything get in his way. Brithon's horse managed to catch up to Praxus.

"When we reach Bantos and his army, Praxus, I want you to know that whatever happens, happens."

"That's fair."

"I know for a fact that Bantos will indeed be present on the battlefield. But, he may have brought himself some form of assistance."

"What kind of assistance would he have?"

"We'll know once we get there."

"I understand."

Riding closer toward the field, in the distance one of Praxus' solders managed to catch a glimpse at the soaring army of Bantos. Pointing ahead, they each stare toward the field and see the soldiers moving in succession with the faint sound of chanting echoing through the air across the mountains of the valley. Praxus stopped and rallied his army to cease their movements. Brithon seeing this had done the same.

"What are they saying?" Praxus asked.

"I can't make it out. I know it's a war cry."

"Hmm. They know we're here. I can see that. Where's Bantos? Can you see him through the mess that is his army?"

Brithon took a gander toward the field in which was before them. The field itself laid near the Bandorian Jungle. A place filled with dwelling creatures of immense size. Although, no sign of the ravenous beasts were seen, Brithon believed Bantos had managed to keep them at bay for the battle ahead. Still looking, Brithon spotted one horsemen suited in armor from his head to his feet. An armor unlike the leather and metal pads which the other soldiers wore. With a single nod, Praxus knew the answer and rode down the valley toward the field as his army followed.

The armies moved with haste to reach the field as Bantos himself saw their arrival. His soldiers chanting had went still. Their hands attached to their swords and spears as Bantos rode forward to meet the opposing armies. Their numbers did not bother the Bandorian king, only amused him for a day of slaughter. Praxus and Brithon reached the field, stopping mere feet in front of Bantos and his army. Praxus' eyes seared with anger and Brithon knew it, waving his hands for Praxus to control himself.

"I am amused and yet surprised you managed to accept this battle." Bantos chuckled. "You even brought yourself some reinforcements. Only goes to show you knew this day would be your last."

"I don't think this day is my end." Brithon replied. "You see, my backup came to me to confront you themselves. Their leader, Praxus seeks to bring a better world for his people."

"His people? And who are his people?"

"Lithonians." Praxus answered boldly. "You massacred many of them during your conflicts of conquest."

"I did what a king would have done. I simply conquered lands suited for the better."

"And killing innocent men, women, and children was part of your conquest? The soldiers weren't enough? The warriors weren't proven enough?"

"Praxus, control yourself." Brithon whispered.

Bantos took a look toward Praxus. His eyes keen as he rubbed his chin.

"Have I done something to you in the past, boy?"

"You've done enough."

"Afraid I haven't. I won't be finished until all kingdoms belong to me. Your friend, Brithon's kingdom is just the next one on my list. Damn Brithrowians nor a pair of savage Lithonians will stop me from my conquest."

Praxus took out his sword, holding it high as his army follows. Dozens of swords for Bantos and his army to see. A grin grew on the face of the Bandorian king as he shouted for his soldiers to attack. The armies went and clashed their blades one o another. Bantos did not flee the battleground as some leaders in times past. This king was deep into the fight, slaughtering Brithrowians and Lithonians with ease. Even for someone of his older age. Praxus moved swiftly through the battlefield, taking out Bandorian soldiers like practice. Their heads slicing off their bodies and falling into the bloody grass. Praxus huffed as he moved with haste toward Bantos.

Over next to where Praxus walked, Brithon fought alongside his soldiers and the Lithonian warriors. The fight became bloodier as the minutes had passed. Praxus sliced his way closer to Bantos as he saw him take out three Lithonians with one blow. An impressive feat even in Praxus' eyes. With the three bodies falling to the ground, Bantos looked up and saw Praxus standing before him. Fire in his eyes. Anger boiling beyond its point.

"I did something to you, didn't I?" Bantos asked.

"You took my mother and father from this life. Robbed me of my heritage."

"Did I? Well, get in line with the others who have said the same and die for their honor."

"The only one dying today is you and your rule!"

"Make it so, savage!"

Praxus with anger in his forefront rushed toward Bantos, swiping his sword against Bantos' own. The two stepped back in the midst of the dying screams and flying sprays of blood across the field. Bantos relished in the moment while Praxus continued to let his anger control him. Stepping with speed and haste, Praxus slammed his sword against Bantos as the Bandorian king deflected the blows and kicked the knee of Praxus, knocking him back before Bantos delivered an elbow swipe to the Lithonian's forehead.

"Your anger. It's getting the better of you. Better get it in place, boy, before you end up killing yourself."

"Enough of your damn talking! Fight me!"

Praxus immediately rose to his feet, his sword in hand facing forward as he stretched out toward Bantos and ended up tapping his sword against Bantos' own. A chuckle echoed from the mouth of the Bandorian king as he shoved Praxus back. A grunt of anger busted from the Lithonia as he went for another strike toward Bantos. The king ducked, only for Praxus to be taken down by a heavy blow. A blow which originated from a war hammer. Bantos nodded with a grin as he looked forward, seeing the wielder of the hammer. A towering figure who stood over the height of three Bandorian soldiers. The hammer itself had to have weighed nearly as one of the Bandorian soldiers.

"Figured you would be here."

"I would do anything for you, my king."

The sound of the battle continued on as Bantos knelt down, checking Praxus' pulse. The Lithonian lives. Bandos sighed as he stood up and sheathed his blade. The hammer wielder looked down at Praxus and raised the hammer.

"Do you wish me to end him?"

"Don't." Bantos. said. "No need in killing the boy. Death is too sweet for him to savor. Living will do the job."

Lowering the hammer, the wielder and Bantos looked out toward the ongoing remains of the battle. Allowing the wielder to enter the fight, he moved and quickly decimated the Lithonians and Brithowians with ease. Their combined efforts could not match the strength of the wielder and his hammer. Within minutes of the fight, Bantos' army had appeared to have won. Seeing the dead bodies of Lithonians and Brithowians on the ground covered in blood. Some without their heads or insides. Bantos saw the day as a victory and rallied his remaining soldiers to return to Bandoria.

Upon their leave, Brithon arose from a pile of bodies with several living soldiers of his own and a few Lithonians who managed to survive.

"Where's Praxus?" Brithon asked. "Where is he?"

Moving through the bodies, they searched the fields for Praxus and were seemly unable to find him. It was as if he vanished from the battlefield without notice. Knowing Praxus is the kind of warrior who would survive the utmost impossible odds, Brithon in his tired state gathered his soldiers and the Lithonians as they agreed to return to his kingdom in hopes of sending out a unit to find Praxus.

Deep in the night, hours after the battle. Praxus awoke and found himself inside of a cave. A cave he was unfamiliar with. In front of him, a fire bellowed. A fire he did not conjure nor make. Attempting to stand on his feet, his back pulsed with pain as he dropped to his knees.

"Do not make a move." said a voice from the darkness of the cave.

"Who's there?" Praxus questioned. "Step into the light and show yourself."

"Is that what you crave?"

"Tell me who you are and why am I here?"

"Very well, Lithonian."

The voice moved from the darkness and into the light. Revealing himself to Praxus. A cloaked being dressed in a violet garb. Yet, like a shadow in his movements. His face unseen, yet a mystic power flowed from his very being. He approached the fire and knelt down in front of it. Siphoning some of the flames into his hands. Transferring the energy of the heat into himself.

"You're a sorcerer." Praxus said.

"Good of you to notice."

"I was taught to abhor those like you. Sorcerers are evil and have only done evil to suit their deeds."

"Such is true for many. Such am I. yet; I will not do the deed of evil this night. For it is not the time."

Praxus sat up and leaned against the cavern walls. Pressing his back against the rocky walls.

"What are you saying?"

"We were destined to meet this night. It was written thousands of years ago and now, it has come to pass."

"Who are you?"

"I am known as Dakin Maul. A sorcerer who desires this world to be in the hands of my kind."

"I've never heard of you."

"You have now. It is destined for us to be mortal enemies. A man of your barbaric stature could only be a perfect match for a sorcerer like myself. A battle for the ages."

"Then, how come you didn't kill me? Why pull me from the battlefield and bring me here?"

"Because it was not your time to die. Not yet."

"So, was it you who hit me?"

"No. that was Roht. A massive warrior who works under the rulership of King Bantos. He's the one who knocked you unconscious and he sought to kill you, but Bantos spared you. Yet, I already knew of this before it happened."

"Enough of this sorcery talk. Why am I here?"

"To heal. You must return to Brithon to reveal your safe and alive."

"I want Bantos. Where is he?"

"He returned to his kingdom as he should. Don't worry yourself, you'll have your moment with him very soon."

"Answer this for me. Since you know the future, tell me. Do I kill Bantos?"

"Yes," Dakin said with a calm voice.

"Do I kill him soon?"

"I will not say. Just know you indeed kill him and save the kingdoms from the tyrant. When you kill him, I will not reveal."

Praxus leaned his head back and pondered on the thoughts. Dakin knew he was pondering as he showed a faint smirk on his face as it could be seen due to the kindling fire beneath him.

"I need to get going."

"You will remain here for the night. Let your body heal and by the morning light, you shall arise and make your way to Brithon continue your journey."

"And where will you be?"

"I'll be around. It is my destiny to observe you. To learn your skill set for our coming battle. A battle of might versus magic."

"I'll be looking forward to it." Praxus said coldly.

Dakin let out an echoing laugh to Praxus' distaste. A laughter one would deem sinister. A cunning laughter.

"I'm sure you will. As for right now, it is best you sleep."

Dakin reached over and tapped his finger on Praxus' forehead, placing him into a deep sleep.

"We will meet again." Dakin said as he moved back into the darkness of the cave.

CHAPTER IV

The next morning had arisen and Praxus had awoken.
Immediately rising to his feet to find Dakin Maul. Hearing no sound
within the cave and the fire which was before him had become a
shallow pile of burnt wood. The peeking light of the sun touched
Praxus' face as he grabbed his sword that was placed against the
cavern walls and made his way out. Upon returning to the outside,
Praxus stared out into the field of decayed bodies. The remains of the
soldiers from the battle before. Their flesh being ripped and torn
apart by the Bandorian birds. Feathers as dark as the night. Talons as
large as a warrior's boot and beaks sharper than the metal one warrior
could wield. There were three of them in the field, yet unaware of
Praxus' movements as he stealthy moved past them to avoid a great
conflict. One which might bring forth his death if Dakin's words
were false.

Praxus took several more steps before he reached the other end of
the field. Taking the final step, he pressed into the ground as he
paused. His quick pause had slid the dirt under his boot, alerting one
of the massive birds. The bird walked toward Praxus as the Lithonia
raised up his sword and pointed it toward the creature. The two
locked eyes as the bird measured Praxus. In such a close range, the
bird stood nearly six feet higher than Praxus. Taking in his scent.
Praxus waited for the right moment to strike and the bird raised up
its head and let out a small cough before turning away and returning
to the dead bodies. Praxus sighed and sheathed his sword, turning
away to leave the fields.

Sometime later, King Brithon rested in his castle back in Brithrow. His men moving back and forth from the doors, giving their king details on the remains of his soldiers and the whereabouts of Praxus. Brithon had hoped Praxus indeed survived the battle as he knew the savage Lithonian had the potential to tear down Bantos' tyrannical rule. As one of the soldiers entered the castle, he came with a sense of urgency. Brithon arose from his seat and faced his soldier. He knew what was to come as he stepped forward and walked outside. Looking ahead toward the kingdom's gates, he saw a horse galloping toward him. The rider as he could tell had come from the field. The closer the rider came, the more he knew. A few more inches the rider rode forward and Brithon showed a smile. A smile of relief and hope.

"He's alive."

Praxus stepped from the horse and greeted Brithon and the soldiers who gathered around. Looking at the soldiers, Praxus even saw some of the Lithonian warriors who stood by his side remaining and they saluted one another as brothers-in-arms. With their greetings, Brithon allowed Praxus into the castle to rest up as he could see the tiredness in his eyes, yet his body was full of energy. Entering the king's throne room, the handmaidens had brought the two men wine to drink. Praxus gulped down the drink within seconds and asked for more to the king's pleasure.

"It is good you survived." Brithon said. "Tell me what happened."

"It was simple. I confronted Bantos on the field. Fought him. I believe I had him defeated until I was struck by a heavy blow."

"Struck by who?"

"A warrior called Roht. I was told he was Bantos' right-hand soldier in his rule."

"Who told you this?"

"A sorcerer who aided me without my knowing. A strange fellow. Called himself Dakin Maul."

"Dakin Maul. That's a name I haven't heard in ages. He's still here and around our region."

"I don't know. When I awoke inside the cave, he was gone. Nowhere to be found."

Brithon sighed as he took a sip of the wine, leaning back in his chair.

"Dakin Maul saved you. That's something I've not known him to do. He must have favor in you."

"Said it wasn't my time to die. That he and I have a battle in the future between my strength and his magic."

"Ah. His prophecies speak once more. He's always been the prophetic kind. Telling those of their futures, only for them to come to pass in a way they did not expect."

"So, he was telling the truth? About our battle to come and that I will kill Bantos?"

"What Dakin Maul speaks is the truth in unrighteousness. Only time will unveil what truth will come of it."

Praxus drank more of the wine. Brithon hesitated to tell him to slow down and avoid becoming drunk in his presence. Praxus respected the king's word and took his time. After a while, Brithon informed Praxus of Bantos' return to Bandoria and how he's seeking to rally more soldiers from other lands to take Brithrow from his hands. Praxus lets out his word that he will kill Bantos and he will not wait years to accomplish the goal. Preparing himself to ride out before nightfall that he would arrive in Bandoria to confront Bantos and kill him before the morning broke. Brithon understood Praxus' motivations and agreed with him.

"What do you need me to do?" Brithon asked.

"I cannot allow you to lead yourself and your men into more danger. Bandoria is full of killers who only slaughter for pleasure. I can sneak in alone and deal with whatever forces come my way."

"You can. Meanwhile, myself and a few soldiers of mine will keep the others busy. To give you time to reach Bantos. I heard he speaks a frequent amount of time in his throne room."

Praxus grinned and nodded, extended his arm toward Brithon.

"Then, it's settled."

The two men agreed to the plan and began making moves. Praxus walked outside and gazed upon the sky, seeing the sun reaching west, he left for Bandoria as Brithon and ten of his soldiers each rode out behind Praxus.

Riding out toward the gates of Bandoria by nightfall, Praxus' anger began to bellow within. Brithon looked ahead and saw the guards standing at the gates. He knew if they could take them out, it would give Praxus a better appointee of entering. Praxus agreed to the plan as he made his way toward the gates, sneaking past them by swimming in the moat around. Brithon and his soldiers approached the two guards at the gated entrance.

"Stop. Identity yourselves."

"We come from Brithrow to deliver news to your beloved King Bantos." Brithon spoke.

"And who might you be?"

"The King of Brithrow."

The soldiers paused themselves as their hands dropped down to their swords. Behind them, Praxus arose from the water as his sword moved through the cool air and slashed greatly with his blade, decapitating the soldiers with ease. Impressing even Brithon and his soldiers.

"You move quick."

"We have no choice." Praxus answered. "Otherwise, we'll all be dead."

The soldiers moved to the gate, opening it for Praxus and themselves to enter. The gate opened with a gentle ease as they looked ahead, seeing the city streets clear of civilians and soldiers. Praxus' eyes looked forward toward the massive palace in the distance. He knew Bantos was there and within.

"I'm going for it."

"Be careful, Lithonian." Brithon said. "We'll handle things out here in case it escalates."

Praxus moved through the city, passing by sleeping soldiers and drunken men who relished in the sight of the whores around them. Bantos saw them as a way of keeping the people under his control and he was right. Praxus knew it to be true, seeing the people had no sign of life within their eyes. Their bodies were living , but their souls were drained. Only the faintest sign and taste of pleasure could keep them at bay. No chance of fighting back against Bantos' power. Looking up toward the steps to reach the palace, Praxus ran forward. Nearly thirty steps he reached without fail.

Standing foot on the palace grounds, he moved quietly to avoid the soldiers who patrolled the area. Using the banners and curtains as his way of moving and hiding, Praxus could hear the soldiers talking amongst themselves. Speaking of the battle prior and hw they wished they kill Brithon and took Brithrow for themselves. Continuing his move deeper into the palace as Brithon and the soldiers inched closer to the palace grounds, Praxus moved as he heard the swift sound of a swinging hammer. Hiding behind the wall, he peeked through the curtain and saw Roht standing in the center of the interior garden to the palace.

"You can quit your hiding, Lithonian." Roht spoke. "My king informed me of your arrival would be soon enough."

Praxus stepped from the wall and walked out through the curtain, facing off against Roht. Seeing him in full. A tall brute. His hammer much larger than his sword. Roht scoffed at the sight of Praxus.

"I could've killed you on the field, yet, my king told me not to."

"His foolish decision and his downfall." Praxus said. "All by his own words."

"I think not. This night it will be you falling before his feet after I pummel you with my hammer. The same hammer which knocked you down before."

"What happened before was a cheap blow. This time, I see clearly. Bantos was my only target this night. However, because of your sneak blow, I'll kill you as well."

"Come then." Roht slammed the hammer. "Give your best blow."

Praxus roared, running toward Roht with his sword swinging.

Roht deflected the metal with his hammer and kicked Praxus in the abdomen, striking him once more with the top of the hammer, causing him to tremble and fall to the marbled floor. Roht laughed, backing away for Praxus to stand up.

"I will not kill a Lithonian while he's on his back. Stand up and face me once more!"

Praxus gripped his sword and showed a smirk, running toward Roht once more as the brute swung the hammer. Praxus saw the coming attack and slid under the weapon, slashing the left leg of Roht with this sword. The pain shot through his lower body as Praxus elbowed Roht in the chest and kicked him in his abdomen. To his dismay, Roht's flesh felt a similar toughness to a bull. Roht stumbled in his steps, yet maintained his balance.

"Should've worn more armor." Praxus said. "Leaving yourselves bare only give you a weakness."

"Yet, you're barely covered in metal."

"I don't need metal to survive. I'm a Lithonian. All we need is leather, furs, and steel."

Roht raised the hammer above Praxus and went for a pummeling slam. Praxus moved from the hammer's path and threw his sword toward Roht. Straightforward, the blade pierced Roht in his chest. Roht looked at the sword in his chest and pulled it out as the blood oozed from the wound. Throwing the sword to the ground, Roht dropped his hammer and cracked his knuckles.

"Fair play." Praxus said, balling up his fists and stomping his feet.

The two swipe attacks onto one another. Praxus delivering several punches to the face of Roht as the brute snatched Praxus by his hair and dragged him across the garden. Taking his head and shoving it into the dirt of the field. Praxus kicked Roht in the wound of his leg and gasped for air as he rose up from the dirt. Praxus grabbed Roht by his beard and returned the favor, holding his head into the dirt before stomping on the back of his head. Roht rose up, shoving Praxus back as he wiped the dirt from his face and spit onto Praxus' chest. A complete show of disrespect to his own humor. Blood pouring from them both. They clashed once again with punches to the face and kicks to the legs. The sound echoed resembled two beasts clashing in the fields. Praxus slowed down to Roht's pleasure and uppercutted the Lithonian to the ground. Praxus took the moment to catch his breath as he heard the laughter coming from Roht.

"They said Lithonians were savages. Bred for battle. Yet, I look at you and wonder if such a tale is true."

Praxus flipped onto his feet and stared Roht in the eyes with a grin.

"The tales are true. I'm their living embodiment."

Praxus leaped onto Roht and pummeled his face, bringing the brute to his knees. Praxus roared as he kicked Roht in the head, causing him to fall to the floor. Praxus paused and looked down at Roht, seeing he's still breathing. Praxus turned away, looking towards the throne room ahead.

"Where are you going?" Roht said coughing. "You'll have to kill me before you face my king."

"I'm here for him. Not you."

"Either way. You die or we all die."

Praxus looked around and retrieved his sword, sheathing it. Roht screamed continually for Praxus to kill him. Praxus went for his sword and paused. Leaving it be. Instead, he turned to the floor and saw Roht's hammer and lifted the massive weapon to Roht's surprise.

"You cannot be that strong. There is no way."

"Yet, you see it before your very eyes. Your time above this ground is finished. Now, go to your gods. Whomever they be."

Praxus raised the hammer and slammed it atop Roht's head to the sound of a cracking whip. A moment of silence moved through the garden as Praxus looked toward his hands and released the hammer from his hands and turned toward the throne room. Walking slowly as he wiped the blood from his face.

CHAPTER V

Praxus took his steps toward the entrance to the throne room. Hearing the beating sound of distant drums and the flowing sensation of water, Praxus looked around him as he saw several waterfalls on the walls. Facing him was the throne seat and within it was Bantos. A chuckle muffled from his mouth as he rose up and applauded the Lithonian for his arrival.

"I knew it wouldn't take you long to defeat Roht. He was a tough warrior in my ranks. However, I've always known his skill could be outwitted by someone of a much quicker speed."

"Roht was not in my sights to kill. I had to take him out to get to you. You're the reason I'm here this night."

"Well then, savage one. Here I am and a sword I hold in my hand. The question is, will you strike me down before I do the same to you?"

"One of us will meet our god this day and I believe it will be you."

"Let's make it so." Bantos grinned.

Bantos swung with a right swing of his sword, clashing the steel against Praxus' own sword. A smile grew on the Lithonian's face as he shoved off Bantos' sword and sliced down toward the Bandorian's abdomen. Stepping back to look, Praxus let out a quick scoff.

"Are you worried? All men bleed."

"You forget, Lithonian. I am not all men." Bantos glared. "I am above all men!"

"Best to show it than to speak it."

The two clashed their blades once more with a more forceful push from Bantos, stumbling Praxus toward one of the waterfalls.

The sound of the flowing waters increased in Praxus' ears as Bantos continued to push him closer. Bantos turned his gaze toward the waterfall and back to Praxus. A thought entered his mind as he let go of Praxus and kicked him into the waterfall. Praxus rose up as the water fell onto him. Stepping forward, Bantos rushed in and grabbed the Lithonian by his neck, holding him down in the water.

"Let's see how long you can live without a moment's breath." Bantos laughed.

Praxus struggled against the might of Bantos. For a man who appeared to be nearly of old age, his strength was of a young man. A peculiar trait in Bandoria. Praxus pushed with his chest, raising up from the water to Bantos' dismay. However, Bantos pressed his boot atop the back of Praxus, shoving him back into the water.

"Just give up." Bantos chuckled. "Accept this death and wander the afterlife with pondering questions of an alternative."

Praxus screamed as the bubbles rose to the surface. With enough strength in him, Praxus shoved off Bantos and arose from the water. His arms stretched and his fists gripped.

"What?" Bantos questioned with fear. "Such strength from a Lithonian is not possible. It is not."

He turned to face Bantos as the Bandorian king went to retrieve his sword from the floor. It was not quick enough as Praxus lunged onto him and pummeled his face in with punches. Praxus continued the blows even as Bantos attempted to block them with his arms and hands. Praxus stood up and kicked Bantos in the chest. Turning back, Praxus went and grabbed his sword and raised it above the neck of Bantos.

"If this is my end, let it be a quick one." Bantos said. "Otherwise, you'll end up dead sooner than I."

"Enough. Your end has come."

Praxus rose up his sword for the kill and setting to make their mark, seven Bandorian soldiers bolted into the throne room with sword sin hand. Without hesitation, they saw their king on the floor and Praxus standing over him with his sword near his neck. The soldiers screamed as they attacked the Lithonian to save their king.

Praxus fought back against the soldiers, swinging his sword to their own surprise. The Bandorian soldiers are used to their enemies quickly submitting when there's more than four. However, such was not possible with Praxus. For his is a Lithonian and Lithonians do not fear numbers. They do not fear anything aside from their own failures and dismays. Praxus gripped the hilt of the sword and impaled one soldier into another. Pressing their bodies against the wall as they fell into one of the waterfalls. Turning to the remaining five, Praxus moved with speed, hacking and slashing his blade against their thighs and forearms. It was within a matter of minutes in which Praxus had slaughtered the soldiers. Their bodies lying on the clear marble floor with the blood pouring through like spilled wine.

"Now to finish you off." Praxus said, turning around to face Bantos.

Bantos was gone. No longer was he lying on the floor within his throne room. Praxus turned around and searched the room with haste. No sign of Bantos caused a yell to echo from Praxus. Sounding off throughout the palace and reaching the peek of the city. Even Brithon and his soldiers heard the roar of the Lithonian.

"I wonder if he accomplished the goal." Brithon said to himself.

Praxus looked at the dead soldiers around him as he could hear the running footsteps of more soldiers incoming. Taking the moment to see the throne seat, Praxus carved a mark into the seat as he made his escape just in time before the soldiers arrived. While the soldiers signaled the city to search for the Lithonian, Praxus had returned to the outside where he was greeted by Brithon and his soldiers.

"Did you do it?" Brithon asked.

"I was close. His men were onto me before I could take the strike."

"So, he still lives."

"Yes. But, not for long. He's wounded."

Hearing the bell sounding as the noise of the rustling civilians began to scream, Praxus and Brithon took their leave. Returning to Brithrow. It was only a matter of days when Bantos sent out the decree for all his soldiers to find Praxus and to bring him to the palace for his sentence. A sentence which would only be death under Bantos' rule. Praxus was informed of the decree by several of his Lithonian spies.

"If he wants me, he'll have to find me." Praxus said. "Or, when I find him."

Elsewhere in the far regions of the land, word had spread of a familiar, yet mysterious weapon was discovered near the hills of the Megarian Mountains. Praxus heard the news and grinned with pleasure. Speaking to his Lithonian brethren, Praxus had set out to uncover this mysterious weapon and plotted to use it against Bantos to bring a full end to his tyranny. Praxus had spoken with Brithon concerning the quest as Brithon had begun to warn him of the dangers which rests near the Megarian Mountains. Threats from giant beasts, savage dwellers, mercenaries seeking challengers, and even the legendary Valley of the Lost. All would bring fear upon a normal man, yet, Praxus of Lithonia was not an ordinary man. He is a man of strength, speed, and valor. Loyal to his cause and to his people and allies.

Praxus had prepared himself for the journey as he gathered his equipment and sharpened his sword. Hearing of more powerful threats which may challenge him only gave him the excitement of a fight. The words of Dakin Maul still lingered in his mind. Their meeting was soon to come if the sorcerer's words were deemed true. That is only something Praxus can ponder on until the time comes. The following morning, Praxus had rode out of the Kingdom of Brithrow and set his travels for the Megarian Mountains. His true journey had just begun.

ABOUT THE AUTHOR

Ty'Ron W. C. Robinson II is the author of several works of fiction.
Including the *Dark Titan Universe Saga* series (*Dark Titan Knights*,
The Resistance Protocol, *Tales of the Scattered*, *Tales of the Numinous*,
Day of Octagon), *The Haunted City Saga* series, and the *Symbolum
Venatores* series.

Also of other books (*Lost in Shadows*, *The Book of The Elect*, *etc.*) and
One-Shot short stories.

More information pertaining to the author and stories can be found at
darktitanentertainment.com.

Twitter: @TyRonRobinsonII

Twitter: @DarkTitan_
Instagram: @darktitanentertainment
Facebook: @DarkTitanEnt
Pinterest: @darktitanentertainment
YouTube: Dark Titan Entertainment

CPSIA information can be obtained
at www.ICGtesting.com
Printed in the USA
BVHW040935011122
650834BV00004B/55